This Precious Gift

by

Paula Lindsay

Dales Large Print Books
Long Preston, North Yorkshire,
England.

British Library Cataloguing in Publication Data.

Lindsay, Paula
  This precious gift.

  A catalogue record for this book is
  available from the British Library

  ISBN 1-85389-985-2 pbk

First published in Great Britain by Wright & Brown, 1959

Cover illustration © Heslop by arrangement with Allied
Artists

The moral right of the author has been asserted

Published in Large Print 2000 by arrangement with Paula
Lindsay

*The characters in this story are entirely fictitious and
no reference to any living person is implied.*

Dales Large Print is an imprint of
Library Magna Books Ltd.
Printed and bound in Great Britain by
T.J. International Ltd., Cornwall, PL28 8RW.

C40380509 +

THIS PRECIOUS GIFT

CHAPTER I

The car slid easily away from the kerb and into the stream of traffic. Judith turned in her seat to wave to the little group of people outside the big white building they had just left. Then she faced back to the road and glanced at the man who sat next to her in the driving seat. He was a handsome man and as Judith studied his profile she felt the familiar lurch of love and longing.

Mark's capable hands rested lightly on the steering-wheel, the gold ring that Judith had given him gleaming in the bright but cold sunshine. He sensed her gaze and turned his head to smile briefly at her.

'That's that!' he exclaimed lightly. Judith nodded. 'Thank goodness it's over,' he added. 'I hate fuss of any kind.'

'There's little fuss attached to a registry office wedding,' Judith retorted and there was a note of sadness behind the words. She looked down at her hands, clasped in her lap. Her wedding ring. The diamonds of her engagement ring flashed and sparkled as she moved her fingers with a restless movement. Her heart was heavy and disappointment swept through her. The ceremony had been brief and cold and she felt that the few unemotional words had made no difference at all to her life. She could not believe that she was now Mark's wife and the despairing thought flashed through her mind that it had all been a mistake, despite the great love she knew for him.

Mark shrugged his broad shoulders. 'I don't see that it makes much difference, my dear. Church or registry office, we're still married in the eyes of the law and that's all that matters.'

A tiny sigh escaped her.

Mark took his eyes from the road for a

brief moment and glanced down at her: his steely grey eyes bore an enigmatic expression. 'Anything wrong?'

She shook her head. 'Nothing at all,' she replied, trying to speak lightly. Not even to Mark could she reveal her disappointment or her lack of happiness.

He returned his eyes to the long ribbon of road that stretched before the car. Traffic was already thinning out a little and the miles slipped by quickly.

'Your father looked a little strained, I thought. Did you notice it, Judith?'

'Yes. He's no longer young and I expect he's working as hard as ever.' It seemed strange to be speaking of mundane matters on her wedding-day: she had expected to know a great joy, a contentment, a glow of romance—but Mark was too practical, too stolid for such romantic ideas.

'Mary looked very attractive,' Mark went on. 'She's a charming person. I'm sure that your father is very happy in his second marriage.'

9

Judith's eyes clouded at the mention of her young stepmother. She had always resented and disliked Mary and even the mature knowledge that her dislike was activated by jealousy could not make her view the young woman in a warmer light. Only courtesy had forced her to invite Mary to the ceremony—that and the knowledge that her father would not attend without his wife. Mark was well aware of the reason for Judith's silence and a sardonic smile touched his lips. 'I'm sorry you don't like Mary,' he said quietly. 'I really think she has great charm.'

'She certainly charmed Father into marrying her,' Judith retorted sullenly, unfairly.

'You're unreasonable,' Mark told her firmly. 'She has a deep affection for your father and he has made her the centre of his world.' He glanced at Judith again. 'My dear, be your age. The days of wicked stepmothers are past. Did you really expect Clifford to spend the rest of his life in lonely solitude? Isn't he entitled to find his happiness where he can?' He added, more quietly, 'Besides, Mary needs him. The whole bottom must have dropped out of her world when her husband was killed—Clifford was very kind to her and he gladly accepted the two children as a condition of their marriage.'

'So Father is saddled with two babies when he has reached the age of peace and quiet!'

Mark laughed. 'Clifford isn't quite in his dotage, Judith!' he exclaimed with amusement. 'As for being saddled, he adores Mandy and Michael.' Sobering, he added, 'I think you should try to conceal your jealousy, my dear, if only for your father's sake. It must grieve him that you and Mary cannot make friends.'

Judith snapped open her handbag and withdrew a slim gold cigarette case. Taking a cigarette, she fumbled among the contents of her bag for a lighter. Mark delved into his pocket and produced his own lighter which he flicked into flame, keeping a steady watch on the road the while. She leaned forward to the light, murmuring an ungracious thanks. She exhaled blue-grey smoke which wreathed up and about her golden head. 'Shall we change the subject?' she asked, when she had recovered her composure, fighting down the flood of jealousy. Mark was always so ready to defend Mary and criticize her for her dislike of the woman.

'As you like,' he returned easily. He glanced at the gold bracelet watch he wore. 'We shall be home in ten minutes,' he said.

Home. The very word sent a thrill of sudden excitement through the woman who sat by his side. In the future, she would share Mark's home, Mark's life, and this thought alone made her feel happier.

She sat up in her seat as the car turned into the winding drive with its green lawns on either side. The house stood expectant and attractive, waiting for their arrival.

Judith had always loved the house and grounds and she knew that her future surroundings would compensate for many things.

As the car drew up outside the big wooden door, Casey came out of the house, his pleasant face wreathed in smiles. He hurried to the car and opened the door for Judith.

'Congratulations and welcome home!' he greeted her warmly, a hand under her elbow to help her out of the car. She smiled up at him.

'Thank you, Casey.'

Mark slammed the door on his side of the car and grinned at Casey.

'May I kiss the bride?' the young man demanded and, without waiting for permission, caught Judith into his arms and kissed her lips lightly. After a brief moment she released herself and Mark moved forward to take her arm, leading her towards the house. Casey stood for a moment by the car, his blue-grey eyes inscrutable, then he hurried after them, tall and lean, untidily dressed in grey slacks and blue sweater, young and eager and light-hearted.

By the door, Mark paused and looked down at his bride. 'I'm not going to be old-fashioned and carry you over the threshold,' he said easily, 'but welcome home, Judith—and be happy, won't you?'

She met his grey eyes and love surged through her being. She nodded, a smile lighting her eyes and touching her lips. 'Yes, Mark, I'll be happy,' she promised and for the moment forgot that she had ever doubted her happiness in the future and the wisdom of her marriage.

Casey hustled them into the lounge. A bright fire blazed in the hearth for despite the sunshine, it was only February and a cold month. Judith drew off her gloves and crossed to the warmth, holding out small, slim hands to the blaze.

'A celebration drink!' announced Casey. 'What have we here?' He crossed to the cabinet and studied the bottles and decanters. 'Well, well!' he exclaimed as if in surprise, 'champagne, by all the saints!' Expertly, he popped the cork and poured the wine. Then, with a theatrical bow, he handed the cork to Judith. 'A souvenir for Madame!' he told her lightly and Judith laughed at him. He was bubbling over with youth and excitement and suddenly she wished that she could share his gaiety. There was no joy in her heart on her wedding-day.

Mark crossed over to the fireplace and pressed the bell. A few moments later, the door opened and his manservant, Alexander, came into the room. Tall, silver-haired and dignified, he had been with Mark for several years. He admired and respected his master and strongly disapproved of his marriage. But he was too good a servant to betray his feelings.

'There you are, Alexander!' Mark exclaimed. 'Come and drink a toast to my wife! Where's Sarah?'

'In the kitchen, sir.' Alexander turned to Judith. 'May I wish you every happiness, madam.' He bowed slightly, deferentially, then turned back to Mark. 'My congratulations, sir.'

Mark accepted the remark with a brief nod of his head. 'Casey, run along and fetch Sarah, will you?' he asked. 'I know she'll appreciate a glass of champagne.'

Sarah was duly forthcoming, bustling along the hall after Casey, her bulky, comfortable body wrapped in a voluminous white apron, her voice lifted in protestations all the way. 'What about my pie? I really shouldn't leave it right now. Don't go so fast, Master Casey—I'm not so young as you think!'

Casey drew Sarah into the lounge, an arm about her massive waist. 'Who cares about pies on a day like this? You must drink a toast to our new bride. Here she is, Mark—have you poured the champagne?'

Judith stood by the fire, her glass in her hand, and she was very sensitive to the

16

atmosphere in the room. Alexander and his wife were resentful of their new mistress and would not welcome changes in the household. They had a great affection for Mark, who stood now with his arm about Sarah's shoulders, encouraging her to empty her wineglass despite her avowals that she was a strict teetotaller and never touched drink of any kind.

'This is an occasion, Sarah—once in a lifetime! You must drink to my happiness in the future. Alexander, another glass?'

The manservant shook his head and respectfully placed his empty glass on a low table. 'Thank you, sir—but you know that I very rarely touch alcohol. If you will excuse me...' He made his departure and a moment later, Sarah insisted that she had to get back to her kitchen and her pie.

Mark moved to the fireplace. Leaning an elbow on the mantlepiece, he looked down at the woman who was now his wife. Her golden head barely came up to his shoulder. She was small with a slim, exquisite figure: the gleaming blonde tresses which owed their beauty solely to nature were drawn back from the delicate features of her face and pinned into a chignon: deep-blue eyes gazed up at him with inquiry in their depths, fringed by long golden lashes. Her generous, sweetly-curved lips were slightly parted. Yet Mark barely noticed her beauty. He anxiously searched her face for some sign of happiness. He could sense the anguish that was within her and could not understand it.

'You make an attractive pair!' Casey broke in, studying them with a smile, his head a little to one side, a cigarette between his fingers. 'You're a lucky man, Mark!' He thrust the cigarette between his lips and inhaled deeply, then stubbed it into an ashtray. 'I expect you've had enough company for a while,' he said lightly. 'I'll take myself off.' He moved towards the door.

'Don't be late for dinner,' Mark said automatically.

Casey grinned, winked at Judith and slipped from the room, closing the door carefully and pointedly behind him. A little chuckle escaped Judith's lips. Then she threw her cigarette into the fire, very conscious of Mark's nearness, her heart missing a beat as he moved slightly. He took her hands in his capable, strong fingers and smiled down at her. Her answering smile was tremulous and uncertain, but her eyes met his steadily. He drew her into his arms and held her close but made no attempt to kiss her. Her cheek was pressed against the roughness of his shoulder. She turned her head and touched his throat with warm, soft lips, seeking the steadily beating pulse, hoping to impart some of her own passion—a heady, emotional passion which swept through her as he held her close to him. He touched her silken hair with his lips and then Judith strained away from him, raised her slight body on tiptoe and pressed her mouth with sudden urgency against the reluctant mouth of her husband. For a moment their lips held, then Mark put her away from him. She looked up at him and her eyes were accusing. Mark touched her cheek with a gentle finger.

'Be patient, my dear,' he said softly. He smiled. Then he turned to the window at the sound of a car and looked out down the drive. 'I thought so,' he said with a hint of resignation. 'Allan and Caroline must have seen us pass—they've come to join in the celebrations!'

Judith joined him at the window and watched the big car sweep up to the house and stop with a screech of brakes. A moment later, Caroline scrambled out of the car and ran up the steps to be followed by her brother. A loud peal on the bell and a peremptory summons by the knocker—and Mark hastened from the room to open the door. A frown creased Judith's brow which was hastily smoothed away as Caroline swept into the room with hands outstretched, a smile lighting her attractive face.

'Darling Judith, we had to come and congratulate you both!' she exclaimed. She held Judith's hands, standing back to survey her with eyes that smiled yet were slightly hostile. 'You look charming, my dear!' she approved.

'I heartily endorse them sentiments!' Allan said from the door and there was real warmth in his eyes and smile as he looked at Judith.

Mark dispensed champagne and for the next few minutes there were congratulations and eager questions and laughter.

Allan and Caroline Mallow were Mark's nearest neighbours and they had grown up together. No one could dispute the relationship between brother and sister. Both had the same shade of auburn hair, twinkling grey-green eyes and fascinating good looks.

Judith liked Allan who was friendly and

pleasant and open in his admiration but she was always aware that Caroline had wanted Mark for herself and resented the intrusion of the newcomer. They were openly friendly but hostility was not far beneath the surface—a fact of which both Mark and Allan were unaware. Casey, with his sensitive reaction to atmosphere, knew and understood the age-old fear and resentment which prevented friendship between the two women.

Having heard the noisy arrival of the Mallows, Casey came down from his room and rejoined the party. When he entered the lounge, Caroline, with her arm linked lightly in Mark's was talking animatedly to him, Allan was crouching on his heels rubbing the ears of Mark's spaniel who had nosed his way into the room, and Judith was standing alone, watching Caroline and Mark. Casey crossed to her side.

'What shameful neglect is this?' he asked, his voice for her ears alone. His eyes searching her face anxiously.

She tilted her chin proudly and smiled. 'I thought you'd gone out,' she replied.

Casey shook his head. 'Do you want some more champagne?' he asked, indicating her empty glass.

'No thank you, Casey. I've had enough for the moment.'

'In more ways than one,' he murmured. 'The vultures weren't slow in arriving, were they?'

A chuckle escaped her. 'Don't be unkind,' she reproved him. 'Mark has just invited them to dinner,' she added with seeming irrelevance.

Casey raised his eyebrows. 'I thought it was a wedding feast, not a wake,' he said lightly. 'Oh well, it's his house!'

Allan rose to his feet and came over to them.

'Hallo, Casey, how are you?' he asked casually. 'I thought you were dining with us last night?'

Casey snapped his fingers in sudden dismay.

'Good lord! So I was—until it slipped my memory.' He glanced at Caroline. 'Am I in disgrace?'

Allan shrugged. 'Caroline said it was to be expected that you'd forget. She invited Sue Barrett as your partner by the way.'

Casey grinned. 'What a miraculous escape!' he exclaimed. 'Didn't Caroline hear that Sue and I had a thumping row the other day? At the moment, we aren't on speaking terms.'

Judith listened idly to the conversation between the two men but her eyes were still on Mark and Caroline, wondering what Caroline could be saying to bring amusement to her husband's eyes and mouth, resentful of their obvious companionship and angry that Mark seemed in no hurry to break up the conversation and return to his bride's side. As though he sensed her scrutiny, Mark turned his head and met her eyes. He smiled slowly but he bent his head a little to catch Caroline's words and Judith turned away without an answering smile. Mark excused himself from Caroline and moved over to Judith. He slipped an arm about her shoulders with a casually possessive movement.

'You're looking a little tired, my dear,' he said. 'Do you want to escape from these madcaps and go up to your room?'

Judith was grateful for the excuse which his words gave her and she nodded. 'Yes, I think I will, Mark,' she replied lightly. She glanced at the slim gold watch on her wrist which had been a present from him.

Allan quickly took the hint. 'We must make a move,' he said, glancing at his own watch. 'Come along, Carol... We'll see you about seven-thirty then, Mark!'

While Mark stood at the main door, bidding his friends farewell, Judith slipped up to her room.

She closed the door behind her and stood leaning against it for a brief moment, listening to the merry crics of the Mallows and the sound of the car engine as Allan revved it into life. As the car drove away down the drive, she moved into the room.

It was large and airy, sunlit at the moment by the rare February sunshine, pleasant and feminine. Mark had told her to choose the colour scheme and the furnishings that she wished, and she had extravagantly complied, the final effect of blue and silver pleasing her eye and good taste.

Judith heard Mark's footsteps on the staircase and heard him enter his bedroom which lay next to her room. A slight feeling of trepidation filled her heart. Mark was now her husband and she loved him—yet she was well aware that love had not prompted him to marry her and she found herself wondering if they could make a success of marriage. What would marriage with Mark entail? There were strange depths to the man that she had never realized. She was doubtful and fearful and unhappy.

Judith stood by her dressing-table with its

silver-backed brushes and soft blue drapes. She looked at the closed connecting door for a long moment. Then she moved and helped herself to a cigarette from a box that lay on a low table. Her hands trembled slightly and her eyes were wet with unshed tears. A tearful bride on her wedding-day, she chided herself, but she could not control her emotions. A fire burned brightly in the hearth and she stared into the glowing depths, a tear escaping to run down her cheek, unheeded.

Angrily, she brushed her hand across her eyes and threw the half-smoked cigarette into the fire. Pride leaped up in her with startling suddenness and she determined that somehow, in some way, she would make a success of this marriage. Surely she could break through the barriers that surrounded Mark's heart and awaken love in him—given time and subtlety, given the patience that her love for him would bring, she would succeed. She knew this and her heart lightened. Mark had his reasons for marrying her and surely affection and tenderness were among them? she asked herself.

Mark was so reserved, so self-sufficient and independent. He seemed incapable of love yet surely passion smouldered beneath his cold manner? With all her heart, Judith yearned to know his love: she was hungry for some sign that she mattered in his life; it was not enough that he had married her—Mark had made it very clear to her that she became his wife for the sake of her love for him.

She ran her fingers through her golden hair, loosening the silken strands from its restraining chignon. Her eyes were anguished for she remembered that night a month ago when they had discussed marriage and his cool, undisturbed voice still rang in her ears.

'You love me very much, Judith,' he had said and it was a statement.

Judith had taken his hand, drawing it

to her cheek and then pressing her lips fervently against his fingers. 'I love you more than anything in the world,' she had replied and her voice was passionate. She had not been ashamed to speak of her love.

'Then you'd better marry me, my dear —if you're sure that's where your happiness lies.'

She had searched his eyes wonderingly, a great hope springing in her heart, joy filling her completely. It was the one thing—the only thing—that she wanted, to be his wife, to call him husband and to share his life with him.

'You want to marry me, Mark?' she had whispered.

'I'm prepared to marry you,' had been his answer and pain had swept through her, 'for the sake of your happiness.'

She had hardly heard the rest of his words.

'You don't love me!' she had accused him.

He had turned away from the look in her eyes.

'No other woman interests me in the slightest,' he had said slowly. Taking out his cigarette case, he had helped himself to a cigarette. Turning it between his strong fingers, he had added: 'I've never loved anyone, Judith. I'm not a great believer in the emotion. I care for you as much as I've ever cared for any woman—and I'm prepared to surrender my freedom in order to marry you.'

What had happened to her pride? Judith asked herself now in wonder, as she had asked herself so many times since that night. Why had she finally agreed to marry him? Why had she never fought against his idea of marriage during the weeks that followed that night? Miserably she reminded herself that she loved Mark—and pride had gone with her heart!

She had loved him from their first meeting.

Her father, Clifford Shaw, had brought

him to their London flat for dinner one night: Mark was the nephew of an old friend who had recently died and the two men had met to discuss the estate, Mark being named as one executor of the will and Clifford as the other. Her father had not then married again and Judith lived happily with him at the flat, attending to the running of their home and organizing of their social life.

Mark had been courteous and pleasant, attentive to the daughter of his co-executor and the perfect guest. Judith had been lovely, poised and intelligent, and the perfect hostess.

She had been fascinated immediately by his dark handsomeness, the bronzed skin, the imposing height and build of the man, the pleasant, cultured voice, the impression of strength which he imparted by his very presence. Meeting his eyes as he glanced up from his coffee as she spoke, her voice had faltered and her heart seemed to stop beating for a brief second. Then he had

31

smiled, she had finished her remark and Mark had turned to her father. But in that moment she knew that she had met the only man she would ever love in her life—the one man who mattered. It had been vitally important that they should meet again—and Mark had sought her out, seeking her company again and again, binding her to him irrevocably with the ties of love as the weeks passed.

She had loved him now for almost a year—but he was still a stranger to her. A stranger who that day had become her husband—because she loved him!

Lost in her thoughts, time passed swiftly, and she was startled when Mark knocked gently on the communicating door and called her name. Quickly, she hurried over and opened the door.

He raised his eyebrows. 'You haven't changed yet?' he queried.

A slight flush stained her cheeks. 'No, I—I... Am I late, Mark?'

He shook his head. A smile quirked

his lips. 'May I not come in, my dear?' Realizing that she barred his entrance, Judith stepped back quickly and the flush was deeper. Mark walked into her bedroom, leaving the door between the rooms ajar. He had changed from his tailored suit into a dressing-gown and a silk scarf was knotted at his throat. He stood with his back to the fire, regarding Judith intently, and she felt her heart lurch as his marked handsomeness shocked her senses in the familiar way. She fiddled with the brushes on the dressing-table, turned away from his scrutiny. 'This is a pleasant room,' he remarked casually. 'It reflects your good taste, Judith.'

'Thank you,' she murmured.

He laughed softly. 'Formality sounds odd on your lips.' He inclined his head to one side in order to catch her eyes in the mirror of the dressing-table. 'What's the matter, Judith? You aren't nervous of me, are you?'

She swung to face him. 'Of course

I'm not!' she exclaimed. His smile was very warm and she thought she detected tenderness in his gaze. She moved to his side with swift eagerness. 'Oh, Mark!' she said softly.

He put his arms about her and she looked up into his face. He gazed into the deep-blue depths of her eyes which revealed so frankly the vastness of her love for him. Suddenly he pressed his cheek against hers, unable to bear the expression of her eyes. 'Don't love too much,' he said against her ear softly. 'Pain lies that way, Judith—it's unwise to give so much of yourself like that!'

She shook her head. 'It's unwise not to give while you have the chance, my darling,' she told him gently. Suddenly she was happy. She drew back a little and laughed into his eyes. 'I do love you, Mark,' she said lightly. 'How wonderful it is to be married to you!'

He released her, brushing back a strand of golden hair from her temple. 'I should wait six months and see if you can still say that,' he told her with a hint of warning in his voice.

'I won't regret marrying you,' she told him carelessly, with a light heart. 'I'll never regret it.'

'Such confidence!' he teased her and he knew that he envied her. Mark wondered how anyone could be so sure that love could last—wondered also how anyone could love with such great intensity. At times it seemed to him that his heart was surrounded by a wall of ice which it was impossible to melt. He was fond of Judith, he enjoyed her company, he admired her beauty and her intelligence, he was glad for her sake to make her happy through marriage—but he lacked understanding of her love for him. Mark had spoken truly when he told Judith that he had never loved any woman...

CHAPTER II

The dining-room was long and low, attractive and pleasant, a bright fire flickered in the hearth at one end of the room. The oval table gleamed in the soft candlelight. Silver and delicate glassware reflected the light. The diamonds on Judith's finger and at her throat sparkled brilliantly.

Mark was handsome and immaculate in evening dress, crisp white shirt and black bow tie. Judith sat on his right, her golden hair sleeked back into its usual chignon, slim and lovely in black velvet. She held her head high, proud and confident in the knowledge that she was Mark's wife. Allan sat next to her and she was conscious of his admiration, his marked attentions. Caroline was in high humour, at times dominating the conversation, very beautiful with her auburn hair gleaming coppery in the soft lighting, green eyes flashing as she turned her head from one to another, vivacious and sophisticated. Casey sat next to Caroline, facing Judith. He was almost a stranger in the formal dinner suit, oddly silent, even aloof—except when he caught Judith's eyes and winked at her mischievously.

Sarah had excelled herself with the meal and Alexander was deferential and unobtrusive, the perfect servant. Fresh champagne had been produced and opened. Towards the end of the meal, Judith wondered if she had taken a little too much wine for she felt heady, excited and talkative.

They rose from the table and went through into the lounge. Alexander brought coffee and Judith handled the heavy silverware and delicate coffee-cups with an ease born of long practice. Mark watched her appreciatively: she would make a wonderful hostess for she was always at her ease and had the happy knack of always appearing really interested in the conversation of her guests. Allan was very impressed by her and he turned to Mark, as they stood together, offering him a cigarette from the slim gold case.

'What excellent taste you have in women, Mark,' he said lightly. 'Judith's exquisite.'

Mark smiled. 'If a man has to marry, then let him search for the best in women,' he replied.

Allan laughed softly. 'A true philosopher,' he retorted. He glanced oddly at his friend. 'I've always imagined that you would take Caroline for a wife one day.'

'So has Caroline,' Mark said. 'Is she very angry with me, Allan?'

Allan shrugged. 'Who knows? Caroline hides her feelings well—and I'm only her brother.'

'She's looking particularly beautiful to-night,' Mark commented. 'What a fabulous person she is, Allan! There seems no end to the variety of personalities she can adopt!'

As though she sensed their discussion, Caroline turned away from Judith and smiled in their direction. She met Mark's eyes and the smile deepened into warm intimacy. Judith looked up at that moment and intercepted the exchange. A tiny pang of jealousy assailed her.

Casey sat down at the grand piano in one corner of the lounge and ran his fingers idly over the keys. It seemed a signal for silence to fall over the room. He began to play, softly, almost to himself and the atmosphere was suddenly charged with tension. Music surged through his fingers and captured the attention of all who listened to him. He did not play any one piece through to the end, wandering from one melody to another, pleasing himself as to choice and apparently oblivious to everything but the music. He had great talent which had never been put to any use other than his own amusement and the entertainment of his friends. Judith sat spellbound, entranced by the music, captivated by the expression in Casey's eyes for he did not glance at the piano keys. He sat with his eyes on Judith's face and it was for her that he played yet no-one knew it but himself.

He stopped playing abruptly and the silence was startling. Then he rose from the piano and helped himself to a cigarette with a casual gesture. He sat down beside Judith. Mark and Allan resumed their conversation. Caroline sat alone, her head back, smoke whirling upwards from the cigarette she held between slim fingers, apart from the others and lost in thought.

Judith touched Casey's hand with an affectionate gesture. 'Thank you,' she said quietly, as though she knew that he had played for her. 'I love to hear you play.'

He looked at her through long dark lashes, oddly, then he nodded. He sighed, exhaling cigarette smoke, conscious of her fingers against his hand, aware of her nearness, and he was suddenly sad.

Judith sensed his need of silence and she sat quietly, her fingers lingered against the warm skin of his hand, her eyes searching the depths of the fire. She had a great affection for Casey and she knew that they were friends. They shared a devotion to Mark and this allied their emotions.

She had wondered at the young man's presence at Mark's home when she first came down to Hurleigh but she had elicited little information from Mark, who seemed to resent her curiosity. But gradually she had discovered that Mark was Casey's guardian—or had been until he reached the age of twenty-one. Then he could have left Hurleigh and made his own life but Casey had preferred to stay on with Mark. Now, at twenty-six, he was perfectly happy, independent of Mark's generosity, and apparently prepared to stay on at Hurleigh for many years to come. If it had occurred to him that Mark and his bride would want the house to themselves, he made no mention of it. Judith knew that she would be glad of his presence, his youth and gaiety, his friendship and easy affection. Casey was only a couple of years older than Judith, he was sensitive and understanding, and they had many interests in common—one of them being their mutual dislike of Caroline Mallow.

Judith glanced at Casey. He had closed his eyes briefly and in the soft light his face had taken on a strange vulnerability, the long dark lashes sweeping his lean, hard cheek, the sensitive mouth in repose, the unruly dark tendrils of hair falling over his brow. He looked younger than twenty-six and he stirred something akin to pity in Judith's heart. Despite their friendship, Casey was such a lonely person, she felt—he was often alone, out on his big black stallion for hours, riding across the open country that surrounded Hurleigh, or walking with his dog Pilgrim, a ferocious and massive Alsatian who obeyed the slightest lift of Casey's finger, or sitting at the piano with his long sensitive fingers straying idly across the keys in haunting melody. He was prey to strange desolate moods—strange because he was normally such a gay and eager young man, bursting with life and merriment.

Sensing her gaze, his eyes suddenly flickered open and she lowered her lashes—but not quickly enough. Stealing a glance at him, she noticed with relief that his expression was one of amusement, slightly mocking, and typical of the man.

Leaping to his feet, Casey went over to the modern and elegant radiogram which stood near the window. He selected some records at random and placed them on the turntable.

'You're a lively lot!' he chided them. 'This is a wedding celebration—or had you all forgotten?'

Once again, music filled the air—this time the strains of a popular hit tune from a recent stage show. Mark moved over to Judith and smiled down at her. 'All right?'

His lips merely framed the words and she nodded briefly. 'I was just talking to Allan about the litter of puppies his red setter bitch has just had—would you like one of them, Judith?'

She raised her eyebrows. 'Another dog, Mark? Don't you think two in the house is enough?'

He shrugged. 'The house is big enough for them all. Allan will save you the best of the litter if you're interested.'

'Perhaps Judith would like to see the pups before she decides,' Allan put in pleasantly. 'They're really very sweet just now.'

'How old are they?' Judith asked with interest.

'Six weeks,' Allan replied. 'Their pedigree is excellent and I'm sure you'll fall in love with them.'

'I'll come along one afternoon to see them,' Judith promised.

'Make it Thursday,' Caroline put in languidly. 'I'm having a few people to tea—they'll be interested to meet you, Judith.' Caroline threw a slightly mocking glance in Mark's direction. 'Few people expected Mark to marry so late—all of us thought him a bachelor for life.'

The merest of flushes touched Judith's cheeks. She wondered again if she only imagined the veiled insolence in the other woman's tone. But she smiled and nodded. 'Thank you Caroline. I'll come on Thursday then.'

'You too, Mark, of course,' added Caroline, running a hand through her auburn curls which were cut in a short and becoming style.

Mark frowned. 'Tea parties aren't in my line, as you very well know. Count me out!'

Caroline shrugged. 'As you wish—but won't it seem rather odd if Judith turns up on her own? Surely you should escort your bride on her first social occasion since her marriage?'

There was a slight pause. Judith glanced

up at Mark, wondering how he would reply to Caroline's remark.

He spoke smoothly at last. 'If that's a reminder of my duties as a husband, Caroline, then I have to thank you for your concern. I'm very new to this game, you know.' Did Judith imagine the trace of annoyance in his pleasant, cultured voice? He added quietly: 'I shall of course disregard my dislike of trivial social occasions and escort Judith on Thursday.'

Caroline raised her eyebrows, a smile playing about her mouth. 'That's a great concession on Mark's part,' she addressed Judith. 'I assure you he would never do as much for me in the past.'

Judith met her eyes squarely. 'I expect the difference lies in our status, Caroline,' she said evenly. 'As Mark's wife, I shall naturally expect him to sacrifice his personal wishes at times—in the same way that I shall co-operate with him. Friendship doesn't always carry the same advantages, does it?'

Caroline's eyes flashed suddenly. It was a rare event for her to be put so neatly in her place.

Casey chuckled. 'Very well put, Judith!' he exclaimed.

To hide her discomfiture, Caroline turned to Mark who stood by her chair, a gleam of amusement in his grey eyes. 'A drink, please, darling,' she requested. He nodded and obediently turned towards the cabinet. Judith watched his easy, lithe movement, the capable hands dealing with the decanters, and noted the smile he threw over his shoulder towards Caroline, in answer to a quip she made. He was strikingly handsome and the blood rushed swiftly through Judith's veins as their eyes met when he handed her a drink. The glance they exchanged held a mutual desire for the evening to end, for their friends to leave, for the man and woman who were newly married to be on their own. Mark shrugged his broad shoulders in the

47

slightest of movements and Judith smiled at him. When all the glasses were refilled, Allan touched Mark's arm and drew him aside for a private conversation. Caroline took the opportunity to turn to Judith with a smile that belied her inner resentment of Mark's wife.

'I still can't believe that Mark is married,' she said lightly. 'He has always seemed to be the ideal bachelor type—so contented with his own company, so independent and self-sufficient. There have been times when I've wondered if he disliked women!' She laughed gently. 'Usually after a flaming row, I must admit.' She glanced sideways at Judith through her long lashes. 'Mark has a terrible temper—but I expect you know that, don't you?'

Judith smiled. 'He hasn't yet lost his temper with me, Caroline. Perhaps you unconsciously annoy him?'

'I think it's rather a case of familiarity breeding contempt,' Caroline said smoothly. 'We've been friends for so many years—we were all children together, you know, Mark and Allan and myself.'

'I expect you regard Mark rather in the light of a brother?' Judith asked with subtle irony in her voice.

Caroline glanced at her sharply. There was more shrewd intelligence in the young girl who had married Mark than Caroline had at first imagined: she was more of a rival than Caroline had thought. So it was to be a fight. She mentally girded her loins and polished her weapons. All her life, Caroline Mallow had been determined that one day she would marry Mark Debenham. It was not her fault that she had reached her early thirties without success—but Mark had always eluded her subtle traps. It was not surprising that his friends should think him settled in his bachelor ways. It was surprising that he should suddenly decide to marry a girl he hardly knew—a stranger to all his friends. Many had been the remarks, overheard by Caroline herself, as to the unexpectedness of his choice. It had been generally assumed by their set that if Mark ever married at all, it would be Caroline who became his wife. Caroline had been convinced of this, too. Bitter disappointment and anger still lurked in her heart and it was not surprising that she should feel so much resentment and jealousy of Judith.

Judith. Caroline studied the young girl who sat so demurely in a corner of the comfortable settee. Hair reflecting the lamplight, gleaming golden. There was a determined lift to the small chin, a hint of firmness about the sweet, gently-curved mouth. Deep-blue eyes looked levelly into the greenish-grey depths of Caroline's lovely eyes. The two women looked at each other and their lack of liking for each other was revealed openly and frankly.

Caroline looked away and helped herself to a cigarette from the box on the table. Judith leaned forward and Caroline picked up the silver, delicate box to offer to her hostess. Judith thanked her with a brief smile and supplied Caroline with a light from the table lighter.

Caroline threw back her head and blew cigarette smoke towards the ceiling. What was lacking in her nature and character and personality that Mark had found in Judith? This was the question which had constantly tormented her since Mark had told her of his decision to marry Judith. At their first meeting, Caroline had unobtrusively studied the girl, trying to answer her own question. She was young—early twenties—perhaps ten years younger than Caroline. But Mark had never known patience for youth. He had never been a youthful person himself—mature and adult when still in his teens, he had despised the silliness of adolescence. It had been Caroline's own maturity which had attracted him then—their mutual liking for so many things, their mutual impatience with discord and ugliness, their mutual intolerance of fools and ditherers—these were a few of the traits which drew them together. But Mark had never seemed to think of Caroline as a woman—and it had piqued and angered her that she failed to stir him to warm emotion. But she had found a rare patience, confident in the knowledge that one day they would marry.

Now she sat facing Mark's wife—and her patience had been wasted, her confidence misplaced...

Caroline passed over the girl's youth. She was lovely—possessing a delicate beauty which must have appealed instinctively to Mark—fair loveliness of gold, blue eyes and pink and white complexion, slender loveliness, small and delicate figure, tiny hands and feet. Yes, all this would have captured Mark's love of beauty. But Caroline had been blessed at her own birth with good looks. Her superb figure had the advantage of height: the auburn hair and grey-green eyes and creamy skin was an ideal combination; her poise and carriage were striking. Their friends had always remarked that Caroline was the perfect foil for Mark's dark handsomeness.

What other assets did Judith possess? A gentle personality mingled sweetness with quiet humour—those were Casey's words and Caroline still knew a surge of annoyance at the description. Casey was a perceptive young man and if he believed that Mark had made an excellent choice in Judith, then was Caroline's determination to win Mark a vain hope from the start? Her eyes hardened and she inhaled deeply on the cigarette. Mark might have married Judith—but marriages could be brought to an end. Caroline was sure that one day Mark would realize his mistake in preferring another woman to the constant companion of his youth and maturity.

Mark and Allan finished their conversation and moved towards the fireplace. Casey turned from the window with a trivial remark and conversation became general.

Casey came to the group and threw

himself down on the thick rug before the fire, his hands linked about his knees. He glanced up and grinned at Judith as she put her hand briefly on his shoulder.

Mark stood behind Caroline's armchair, his hands resting on the high winged back. Judith noticed that the woman was disturbed by Mark's proximity, although she covered it with a brittle sophistication and easy conversation.

It was very late before the Mallows finally made their farewells and departed. Mark waved them off from the stone terrace which ran along the length of the lounge, overlooking the lawns and drive.

Judith turned to Casey, who stood by the hearth, watching the play of expressions on her lovely face.

'You don't like Caroline Mallow,' he stated.

Judith looked at him quickly, startled, then she smiled a little guiltily. 'Is it so obvious, Casey?'

He shook his head. 'I look for the

signs,' he assured her. 'You're both very subtle—the occasional barbed remark—a quick, calculating glance—a brief challenge. I don't particularly care for Caroline, either. I think the dislike is mutual—but Caroline's like that. She would never waste her affections on someone who doesn't care for her...'

'Surely you're mistaken there?' Judith said quickly. 'You've forgotten Mark!'

'You're so sure that Mark doesn't care for her?' he asked diffidently. 'You're probably right...'

'What do you mean, Casey?' she asked quickly, a little unsteadily.

He shook his head. 'They've been friends for a long time,' he said slowly. He grinned. 'It isn't surprising that she isn't exactly enamoured of you, Judith. How would you feel if some young girl came along and took away the prize you'd been baiting for over a period of years? After all, let's face it ... Caroline Mallow is over thirty and she's wanted Mark since she was in her teens.

She's turned down good offers in the hope that he'd finally want to get married—and she was confident he'd want her when the time came. Now he's married you—much to everyone's surprise—and Caroline will have to look to her face-packs if she wants a husband other than Mark!'

Judith chuckled but she tapped his arm sharply.

'You can be a beast, Casey,' she told him with reproof in her tone. 'She's really very beautiful.'

Taking her hand, Casey lifted it to his lips and kissed the fingers gently. 'She can't hold a candle to you, my sweet!' he murmured lightly. Judith smiled and released her fingers, pausing only to touch his cheek in a brief caress before she turned to the window as Mark entered from the terrace.

Mark shivered slightly. 'It's a damn cold night!' he announced. He crossed to the decanters. 'A last drink, Casey?'

Casey shook his head. 'No thanks. I'm

going to bed.' He yawned. 'I won't see you at breakfast—I'm hunting with the Ancells and it's an early start.'

'Be careful,' Mark warned. 'The ground will be like iron in the morning.'

'It's time you stopped worrying about me,' Casey retorted. 'This won't be my first hunt, you know,' he added with sarcasm. 'Good night, Judith.' He winked at her from the doorway. 'Good night, Mark, old man...' He closed the door behind him and they heard him whistling blithely as he made his way up the broad staircase.

Mark studied the wine in his glass. Then he looked across at Judith. His eyes were enigmatic. 'Well, did you enjoy the evening?'

She knew that with Casey she could always be truthful and that he would never condemn her for the way she felt. But she found it necessary to deceive the man she loved. 'It was most entertaining,' she replied brightly.

He nodded. 'Good.' He swirled the wine in his glass, then drank it and put the glass down. He moved to join her by the fireplace. 'I'm very fond of Casey,' he said abruptly. 'He's impressionable and sensitive and emotional—don't encourage him too much, Judith. I don't want him mooning about the place with a broken heart!'

She stared at him in surprise. 'I don't really understand you, Mark.'

'I think you do,' he said curtly. 'It's obvious that Casey is already fond of you...'

'I'm fond of him,' she retorted eagerly. 'But it means nothing, Mark!'

'At the moment,' he amended. 'Perhaps never on your side—but Casey is likeable, gay, good-looking.'

Judith faced him squarely. 'What are you leading up to, Mark?'

He looked down at her for a long moment. Then he said slowly: 'I just want to make things clear to you, my dear.' He was very serious and her eyes narrowed in inquiry. 'I'm old-fashioned where marriage is concerned, Judith,' he went on, choosing his words carefully. 'Perhaps that's why I've never rushed into it before. I believe that it's a step which is final and binding—and it would be useless for either of us to have regrets.' As she moved, her lips parted to speak, he placed a hand on her shoulder. 'No, wait a minute, Judith. I know what you want to say—that you'll never regret marrying me.' She smiled softly and nodded. 'That's how you feel on your wedding-day—a very natural emotion. But the years could make a difference to your feelings—you might meet someone else who matters in your life—someone who represents more happiness than I can give you. I'll tell you now, Judith—so you will never entertain false hopes ... I'll never give you your freedom. You're my wife until death comes between us...'

There was silence while Judith looked up

at him, trying to phrase the question that was in her heart. At last she said slowly, 'And if you found someone else...?'

He shook his head. 'Then I should have to put her out of my life.' He smiled briefly. 'It isn't likely that such a situation will ever arise. I've reached the age of thirty-five without suffering the pangs of love, Judith—I imagine myself to be fairly immune by now. But you're young and emotional—men admire you, I've noticed ... you're entitled to choose your friends and spend your time how and where you please. I don't like the idea of petty ties—I won't be a demanding husband, my dear—as long as you never forget the one tie that binds you. Never forget that you're my wife. I demand loyalty from you, if nothing else.'

Judith turned towards the dying fire. Her thoughts were in turmoil. Was it possible that this was Mark, her husband, saying such things to her? Was he so blind to the depths of her love for him? Was he so insensitive that he didn't realize the cruelty of his words on this day of all days? Her eyes were hard as she stared into the glowing embers. So Mark considered himself immune from love? She was even more determined to win his heart, to break his pride, to bereft him of his self-sufficiency.

Quietly she said: 'You don't love me, Mark.' She had never realized before how true this was: he had never spoken of love to her but she had thought him reserved, a little cold, forgiving him because she loved him, confident that marriage would change everything. 'Why did you marry me?' she asked, needing to know yet dreading his reply.

His answer came without hesitation. 'Because I needed a wife to run my home, to act as hostess when I entertain, and to be a companion for me when I want one. Because I felt I had remained a lonely bachelor long enough.'

'Is that all?' Judith was pale and her

eyes were dark with pain yet her chin lifted proudly.

Mark put a cigarette between his lips and flicked his lighter into life. Then he tilted his head back and blew smoke into the air before he replied. He said slowly: 'I knew you loved me—it was an added advantage, in my opinion. You resented your father's second marriage and refused to make your home with Clifford and Mary—marrying me solved the problem of where you were to live. Clifford hated the thought of you living alone in a London flat.' He tilted her chin with a finger and looked into her strained eyes. 'Tell me, Judith—what reasons did you credit me with? Love? I've never deceived you on that point. Passion? That would be a poor basis for marriage. Money? That doesn't enter into it for I have plenty of my own. Companionship? As good a reason as any, surely.'

He raised his hand to touch her hair, running his fingers over the silken sheen of gold. Judith stood quiescent under his touch but her slim body trembled and she was filled with quiet despair and pain. He slipped an arm about her shoulders and drew her against him, holding her close. She was very conscious of the subtle strength in his powerful body.

'It sounds much like a business arrangement,' she said finally, slowly.

He nodded. 'Marriage is a partnership, after all, isn't it? One wouldn't enter into a business partnership without due and careful consideration to bear where marriage is concerned?'

'Yes, if one can be so unemotional about it,' Judith replied, forcing her voice to evenness. There was a trace of bitterness behind the words.

'I'm not a very emotional person,' Mark admitted candidly. 'There isn't much romance in my soul—I thought you knew that, Judith. As a woman, you look upon marriage as the romantic union between lovers. I'm more practical—I think

63

of it as a partnership for life and therefore I chose my partner with great care and forethought.'

'Should I be grateful that I qualified for the exalted position of your wife, Mark?' Judith's voice held a note of deep irony.

Mark sighed. How difficult it was for Judith to understand and he regretted now that he had ever embarked upon explanations of his actions. He realized that her feelings were hurt. Caroline would understand and agree—they had discussed the conception of marriage so many times—but Mark had wanted Judith for his wife. He smiled ruefully. 'Don't be angry with me,' he asked quietly. 'Surely you prefer to hear the truth, my dear? Would you rather I deceived you and pretended to a love I don't feel?'

Judith was doubtful on this point. As an integral person, she admired and respected the truth—yet she could not resist a tiny prickling thought that she would be much happier if she could deceive herself that

Mark loved her. Eventually, she shook her head. 'I've always known in my heart that you don't love me, Mark—I hate pretence but I'm sorry that I leave you so completely unmoved.' She smiled sadly. 'It isn't much of a compliment to my charms, is it?'

'Unmoved?' he repeated. 'I have a very great affection for you, Judith. Unmoved?' he said again. He laughed softly. Leaning forward, he touched her forehead with his lips, then ran his mouth to her eyes, her cheeks, the proudly-lifted chin—finally he kissed her parted lips, softly, gently, sensing the instinctive response which was her love for him. He felt passion flowing through his veins and he caught her closer to him. His wife ... his young and lovely bride ... his partner for the rest of his life.

CHAPTER III

Judith tried hard to conceal her dislike of Caroline Mallow. Mark obviously wanted the two women to be friends and he encouraged Caroline to spend a great deal of time at his house.

'We've been friends for a long time,' he explained to Judith. 'People will be only too ready to gossip if they discover that she isn't welcomed at my house by my wife.'

Judith looked at Mark quickly. 'Then you know that I don't like her?'

He nodded. 'I know—and Caroline knows. But she will persevere in winning your friendship. It means a lot to her, Judith.'

'Why should it?' she demanded, disbelievingly.

Mark spread his hands in a small gesture.

'I'm very fond of Caroline—I think she's fond of me. It's only natural after all these years. She tells me how much it upsets her that my wife dislikes and resents her...'

Judith interrupted sharply: 'Caroline told you that!'

'Yes. I can understand how she feels. I wish you'd make the effort, my dear.' He smiled at her. 'I think there's a little jealousy in you, isn't there? Is that why you find it so hard to make friends with Caroline? I assure you there isn't any reason why you should be jealous. We've never been more than good friends.'

'Really?' Judith said quietly. 'I dare say I misunderstood the situation.' As Caroline had meant her to misunderstand, she thought to herself, remembering the subtle hints, the little reminders of the 'friendship' of old standing which existed between her husband and Caroline.

Judith looked up at Mark. He wore disreputable old grey flannels and a fawn sweater. Over the sweater he wore a leather jerkin. His cheeks glowed with good health and vitality, his dark hair fell over his brow where the strong wind had caught it and ruffled the sleek locks into curls. He had been exercising the dogs and had just a few moments ago entered the lounge from the terrace with them at his heels. A casual remark that he had invited Caroline to ride with them early the next morning had sparked off their conversation. Judith resented the invitation. She adored riding and often she thought that her early morning ride with Mark was the happiest focal point of her whole day. Even Casey never intruded on their privacy at this time—yet Mark had invited Caroline Mallow without consultation with her. She hid her annoyance and it melted as she looked up at him, admiring his glowing good looks, proud of the man who was her husband, her love for him as strong as ever despite the disappointment she often suffered, despite her failure to sense some flicker of response to her love in their association. They had been married for almost a month. She was happy enough when she did not analyse her happiness too closely. She tried to fill her time from morning to night, knowing that once she gave herself time to think and regret and yearn, her life would seem barren and empty.

Mark was normally an active man yet this past month he had spent lazily and contentedly at Hurleigh. It had seemed pleasant to ride and walk with Judith; to escort her to the homes of various friends for dinner, luncheon, cocktails, parties; to hunt with the Ancells who had taken a liking to Mark Debenham's young wife and who frequently invited them over to the Hall. He had enjoyed entertaining at the Lodge, proud of Judith's poise and charm, glad of the opportunity to show off his new possession. She ran his home very well, managed Alexander and Sarah with tact and consideration, made no secret of her pleasure in the Lodge and the surrounding grounds, was a willing companion in all his activities, and always looked lovely, well-groomed, well-dressed, happy and healthy. Mark was satisfied with his marriage and assumed that Judith had settled down happily to the idea of being his wife.

Since she had married Mark, Judith seemed to grow more radiantly lovely each day. She blossomed into rich maturity. She developed a new confidence and gave the impression of inner serenity. Because she was determined to find happiness in the strange marriage she had made, Judith suppressed all doubts and longings, reminding herself that even if Mark did not love her, at least she was his wife and that fact alone should bring her happiness. No other woman could claim her position. Though Caroline might purr and spit her feline observations, making little or no attempt to hide her jealousy and hostility when the two women were alone, Judith held the ace card. She had married the man Caroline wanted and she was secure in this knowledge.

Mark was not a demanding husband. Sometimes Judith wondered if there was a lazy streak in his nature that she had not suspected or met before. He seemed perfectly content to lead an inactive, lazy existence at Hurleigh for the time being. He made few demands on her time. It had been Judith's suggestion that they should ride in the early mornings and he had agreed readily. But this was their only definite hour together. They made separate arrangements for the rest of the day. Occasionally Judith would check with him that he was free to dine or lunch or drink cocktails or make up a party to invade London's night-clubs. Sometimes he would ask her if she cared to accept a certain invitation or preferred a quiet evening at home by themselves.

He was not demonstrative. His rare caresses were precious to Judith because of their rarity. She would not force herself to his attention although there were times when she longed to put her arms around him and rest her cheek against his, when she yearned to touch his hair, his smooth cheek, the attractive cleft in his chin, with her lips. Sometimes the desire to hold him close swept through her with startling intensity. It could be prompted by a mere sideways glance of his grey eyes through long dark lashes, a subtle curving of his lips in a smile that was meant for her alone, or an accidental brushing of their hands when he gave her a cigarette or a glass or a letter that he wanted her to read. She was weak because of her love for him yet not so weak that she would betray her need of his arms, his lips and the strong, masculine body with its hidden strength. Seldom did he kiss her and rarely did he take her into his arms: the nights they spent together had been few during the last month, yet recalling his passion, his embraces, the swift urgency of his need, could send the blood rushing through Judith's veins, could make her heart stumble violently and miss its beat, could make her slim body tremble when he stood close to her. Yet Mark seemed oblivious to the effect he had on his wife. He did not realize her constant and desperate need of him, the longing to know his love as well as the passion which could possess him briefly.

Mark threw himself into a comfortable armchair and crossed his long legs. He brought out his cigarette case and opened it. Then he frowned.

'Damn! I've run out of cigarettes. I meant to get some in the village.' He sat up and leaned forward to open the silver box that lay on the table.

'That's empty too,' Judith told him. She indicated the cigarette she held between her slender fingers. 'This was the last.' She stood up and went over to him, twisting the cigarette, handing it to him. 'Finish it for me, Mark.'

He shook his head. 'No. I expect Casey has some. Alexander should have plenty in stock—this is ridiculous. Supposing we had friends in for a drink—and couldn't offer them a cigarette!' He was visibly annoyed.

Judith looked at him in surprise. 'Such a little thing to be annoyed about, Mark,' she said quietly.

'You must have known they were getting low,' he snapped in reply. 'Surely you could have spoken to Alexander about it?'

She flushed a little. 'Drinks and cigarettes are your province, Mark—I thought we'd agreed on that.' She strolled towards the door. 'I must change. I'm going with Casey into Town. I'll get some cigarettes while I'm there.'

'Put something warm on,' Mark replied automatically, his anger fading as it always did when met by Judith's cool composure. 'It's very cold out.'

She closed the door quietly behind her. Mark sat sprawled in his armchair for a moment. Then he picked up a heavy iron poker and broke up the thick logs which came from the estate and gave the Lodge its wonderful, warm, attractive fires. At the sound of the poker against the wood, the spaniel Digger looked up, ears too heavy to raise properly, his eyes searching Mark's face eagerly and anxiously. Mark bent down to rub the dog's nose and ears. Digger was an old friend, getting fat and lazy now, but still faithful to his master.

The door opened and Casey came into the room.

'Judith tells me you want a cigarette—and the box is empty,' he said lightly. He flicked open his own slim gold case and offered it to his one-time guardian. Mark thanked him and took a cigarette. Casey also took one, turning it between his long, sensitive and nicotine-stained fingers. He seemed in no hurry to light the cigarette. He looked down at Mark and his eyes were a little anxious. He moved as if to speak—and then changed his mind and bent to fondle Digger. He was dressed in an expensively-tailored, immaculate blue suit, very pale blue shirt and darker blue tie. His dark hair waved sleekly back from his intelligent brow and he had obviously taken pains with a recent shave.

Mark flicked the table lighter into life and Casey bent his head over the flame with a murmured words of thanks.

'What's up, Casey?' Mark asked softly. He knew the young man very well—and he knew when something troubled him.

Casey thrust his hands in his pockets and stood with his back to the blazing logs. 'I can't hide anything from you, can I, Mark?' he said ruefullly.

'Why should you want to hide things from me?' Mark countered. 'No matter what you do—at any time—I'll never condemn you for it. I'll always help you, Casey—you know that.'

'I don't think you can help this time,' Casey replied quietly. 'It's something I must thrash out on my own.'

Mark rose to his feet. He crossed over to the french window and looked out. It was a grey day and snow was just beginning to fall. Mark waited a long moment and his heart was heavy for he knew the cause of Casey's depression. It had been apparent for some days past. He had sought his own company more and more, almost deliberately avoiding Mark and Mark's wife.

He said evenly: 'You know, I'm supposed to go to Paris next week. I had a letter from Marcel and he says it's time I visited them. I'm not very keen on leaving Hurleigh just now.' He turned and looked at Casey. 'Do you blame me? This is the longest rest I've had in my life and I'm enjoying it. Would you like to fly over to Paris for me, Casey? You've done so before—you know the set-up—have a few days there and enjoy yourself!'

Casey met his eyes squarely. 'You want me to run away from things, Mark? That doesn't sound like the kind of advice you usually give me. I can think of a better solution. You go to Paris and take Judith with you. She may be happy here but what sort of a honeymoon has it been for a girl with as much romance in her heart as she has?'

Mark pursed his lips and pulled at them with his fingers thoughtfully. 'I suggested Paris as a break for you, Casey. What will you do here if Judith and I go away for a few days?'

Casey laughed. 'I'm not a child, old man. I can arrange my own entertainment.' Judith entered the room and he turned to her eagerly. 'You'd like a few days in Paris, wouldn't you, Judy?'

'Paris? What's all this about?' she replied laughingly. She had changed into a tweed suit of royal blue which emphasized her slim fairness. 'Who's going to Paris?'

Mark explained briefly: 'I have to go over on business. It occurred to me that you might like to come with me.'

She hesitated a moment. 'I prefer Paris in the Spring,' she said slowly. 'It always depresses me in the winter-time—so grey and cold. Just like London.'

Mark shrugged. 'It's up to you, dear. I offered the trip to Casey but he prefers to remain buried at Hurleigh.'

'May I think about it, Mark? I don't have to make up my mind at this moment, do I?'

He shook his head. 'I must make all arrangements by Friday,' he replied. 'So let me know as soon as you can, Judith.'

Judith turned to Casey. 'Are you ready? I don't want to miss any of the matinée—I'm looking forward to it so much.' She threw a smile at Mark. 'I wish you enjoyed the theatre more, Mark...'

'I couldn't sit through a frivolous omelette like *Singing Angels*,' Mark retorted. 'I've little patience with that kind of thing—it's more suited to romantic youngsters like you and Casey. Enjoy it, won't you!'

'We'll probably stay in Town for the evening,' Casey told him. 'Why not drive up and join us later?'

Mark smiled. 'No thanks. I'm going to

have a quiet evening.'

In the car, Judith turned to Casey and tucked her gloved hand into his arm. He smiled down at her briefly and then turned his dark eyes to the road, concentrating on driving the big saloon. He preferred his small, open sports car but the weather was too cold and even Judith's mink coat would not have been sufficient protection.

'I wish Mark were more enthusiastic about the things we enjoy, Casey,' she said with a little sigh. 'I love to dance till dawn. I love night-clubs, parties, the theatre—but I think Mark disapproves at times. I can't help loving life!'

'That's because you're young, Judy,' he told her gently. Casey was the only one to shorten her given name and she liked the soft, pliable *Judy*.

'Because we're young,' she corrected. She laughed up at him. 'How glad I am that I have you to be young with, Casey. You're such fun—and Mark can be such a sobersides! Poor old Mark!' she added and then stopped short. The sobriquet seemed cruel and incongruous for she never thought of Mark as old, despite the twelve years that separated their ages. He was certainly far from poor, she thought. She would have starved with Mark in a garret, if necessary—but it would never be necessary for Mark had an ample private income as well as the money which came in from the art galleries he ran in London, Rome and Paris, having taken over from his father and grandfather before him. Debenhams was a famous name in the art treasures world. To hear it mentioned by strangers or friends, to see the name above the gallery in Bond Street, to read of some fabulous piece which had just been added to the collections—all these gave Judith a proud little thrill, as though she had been personally responsible for the existence of Debenhams. She supposed it was because of her love for Mark. She was very proud of his background, his heritage, and the impact of his name and personality on complete strangers.

She fell silent, feeling a little disloyal to Mark because of her criticism. Yet she knew that Casey would understand how she felt and know her words to be spoken lightly.

In the theatre, her eager young face turned to the spotlit stage, lips slightly parted, her laughter coming easily and often, she held Casey's hand. He was aware of her nearness, reminded frequently by the swift pressure of her fingers when she wanted him to share an amusing moment, by the swift glance she gave him from laughing eyes. Casey barely followed the successful comedy. He could not concentrate on the dialogue when Judith was so near him in the dimly-lit auditorium. His senses were disturbed, his lips dry and warm, his heart beating heavily, a queer fluttering in the region of his stomach when she turned to smile or whisper to him.

He was not only too conscious of

Judith's loveliness and nearness: he could not forget that she was Mark's wife. Mark was everything to him. He owed him too much to betray his trust and friendship. Mark was more than a brother; more than a father, more than a friend. Casey had always adored and idolized him. He had been glad to befriend the girl Mark had chosen for his wife because he knew that it would please him. But it had been easy—fatally easy—to allow friendship to pass the boundaries of mere friendship, to fall gently and sweetly in love with her deep-blue eyes, the swing of heavy golden hair, the tilt of her chin, the warm, eager smile, the grace and ease of movement, the husky voice with the attractive lilt. Casey loved—and was miserable because he could not speak of his love, could never possess the woman he wanted, could never betray Mark. He was miserable because he found it difficult to be with Judith and hide his emotions, to stop himself folding her into his arms and drowning in the sweetness of her lips. It meant a constant guard on his tongue, on his body, on his eyes—and Casey found the strain almost intolerable. Yet he could not willingly tear himself away from the nearness of her. He tortured himself daily with her company. Deliberate avoidance of her was too much pain and misery—unnecessary suffering. At least, when he was with her, he knew her gentleness, her sweet consideration, her tender affection, her light-hearted chatter and husky laugh, her swift humour... It seemed to the man who loved her that Judith had no faults and he would have been astounded to know that the man she had married carried no love for her in his heart. But Judith kept her secret well—and Casey knew how undemonstrative Mark had always been, how reserved and cold, but with depths of fire and passion seldom seen. It was natural that Casey should assume that Judith knew of the man behind the façade that Mark showed to the world.

Mark sat for some time before the fire in the lounge. Casey had left some cigarettes in the silver box and Mark steadily smoked these, his gaze riveted on the blazing depths of the fire, his thoughts busy with the Paris gallery, Marcel's letter, Casey's infatuation for Judith in which no one could help him, the lack of cigarettes in the house, his meeting with Caroline when he was out with the dogs...

They had almost collided as Mark rounded a corner of the high wall which surrounded the grounds of the Lodge. Caroline had put a quick hand on his arm to steady herself, laughing.

'How impetuous you are, Mark!' She bent for a moment to caress the dogs who knew and welcomed her gladly. Then she straightened and smiled into his eyes. 'You're looking very fit and very handsome, my dear. Married life seems to agree with you.'

Mark nodded. 'I should have tried it years ago,' he said lightly. 'But I don't regret my years of freedom—they were very pleasant, on the whole.'

'Yes, we had some good times.' Her voice was a little nostalgic. 'Do you remember, Mark—how we used to meet at six in the morning and ride over the hills and far away! What wonderful times they were!'

'I still ride at six in the morning,' he told her, smiling. 'Judith is an early riser, fortunately—so we ride together.'

A look of anger flashed into her grey-green eyes but escaped Mark's notice. 'I think that's charming,' she said warmly. 'I've always believed that married couples should share the same pleasures. We had so many things in common, Mark, always—' She laughed softly. 'Perhaps we should have married, my dear—I swear I'd have made you happy!' There was an intensity behind her words that reached him and, not for the first time, he was aware that more than affection and friendship existed in her feeling for him.

He squeezed her fingers. 'Life plays strange tricks, Caroline,' he said slowly. 'If we had married, I doubt if we'd have found happiness—we know each other too well.'

'I don't consider that a drawback,' Caroline retorted swiftly.

'Which is the point at which we always differ, Caroline,' he told her with a smile. The dogs were growing impatient, running on and then back to sniff at his feet. He looked down at them. 'Don't you think it's rather silly to harp on the past, my dear?' he asked coolly.

She flushed. 'I should feel happier about your marriage if I thought Judith wanted my friendship,' she said ruefully.

This made Mark glance up sharply. 'I thought you got on quite well?' he asked.

She shook her head. 'I'm afraid Judith doesn't like me, for some reason or other. Do you think she's jealous that we've been friends for such a long time, Mark? I'm sure if the position were reversed, I would feel just the same.' She glanced at him through long lashes.

'I can't imagine you suffering from petty jealousy,' he retorted immediately. 'You're too fine a person, Caroline. I don't think Judith is jealous of you. I think she's a little shy—and perhaps the few years that separate your ages influence her reluctance to make friends with you.'

Caroline's eyes flashed. But he had said *'few'* and she didn't intend to remind him that Judith was ten years her junior! Thirty-three! Resentment flared in her again at the thought. She had waited all these years for Mark only to be spurned in favour of a chit of a girl—why on earth had Mark married her? What had he seen in her? If he could not love *her*, argued Caroline, what then did *Judith* possess that she was able to win him so easily?

'I hate to think that I cannot get along with your wife, Mark,' she said at last. 'After all, we have something in common.'

Mark raised an eyebrow in query. 'What's that?'

'Your happiness at heart,' she returned easily.

Mark smiled, his eyes alight with sincere warmth. 'You're very sweet, Caroline,' he told her. Suddenly he drew her to him and kissed her cheek. 'I want you and Judith to be friends,' he said emphatically. 'There isn't any reason why you should dislike each other!'

'I don't dislike Judith,' Caroline protested swiftly. 'I think she's charming, very pretty, and very sweet.'

'I think it's only shyness on her part that prevents your friendship,' Mark said firmly. 'Why don't you ride with us in the morning, Caroline? The more time you spend together, the easier you'll break the ice!'

Caroline nodded, well pleased. 'Six o'clock?'

'Six o'clock it is—at the Lodge Gate.' He grinned at her. 'I must be off, Caro—these brutes are impatient.' The nickname dated from their childhood days but he seldom used it now. The fact that he did so at this moment proved that she had convinced him of her distress that she and Judith could not be friends. It was a word of comfort and a promise that he would see that all was well eventually.

She watched him walk on towards the Lodge, tall, powerfully-built, his muscles rippling beneath the leather jacket, his dark head high, his body thrust against the icy wind which swept around the corner. Caroline drew her furs closer about her and went on her way...

For such an intelligent man, Mark was obtuse where Caroline was concerned. Yet he claimed that he knew her too well. He could not see through her subtlety. He did not realize that a spurned woman is a dangerous one and that Caroline had a clever tongue which could be turned to her own purposes. He firmly believed her claim that the hostility was all on

Judith's side and he was annoyed that his wife could not hide her dislike of his friend. Despite his knowledge that Caroline had loved and wanted him for years, he would not admit her capable of jealousy because he had married another woman. He credited her with a fineness she did not possess but Caroline was a clever actress and had always baffled him by the sudden changes in her personality. He had seen so many sides to her nature that he found it difficult now to decide which was the real Caroline—there had been times when she had said and done things alien to her real character in order to confuse him further. Mark was aware of this but it had only amused him—because that was just Caroline's way and nothing would change her.

He was roused from his thoughts by Alexander who came in to replenish the fire with fresh logs, switch on the lamps and clear away ash-trays and used glasses, tidy cushions and pull the heavy drapes which shut out the gloom of the early dusk.

'Will Mrs Debenham and Mr Casey be in to dinner, sir?' Alexander asked respectfully.

'No. I shall be dining alone, Alexander.' His reply was curt. He sensed a faint disapproval in his manservant's tone of voice. Perhaps it seemed strange to Alexander and Sarah that he should be alone by the fire when his bride of a month was out with Casey for the evening—Mark shrugged mentally. He did not deny Judith any kind of pleasure. On the day they were married he had made it clear that her time was her own, that she could choose her own entertainment and her own company. He relied on her discretion and common sense to the full. He knew that she was to be trusted: no one would ever be able to create a scandal out of his wife's activities.

Thinking of Judith, his eyes softened and he felt a familiar sensation of warmth creep over him. He smiled to himself, his dark and handsome features bathed in the soft lamplight.

How lovely she was. Not only in looks but in character. One was aware of the sweetness, the generosity, the capacity for loving that lived within her at every turn. She was patient with him, accepting the fact that he lacked romance, forgiving him for the coldness which was part of his nature. He might often hurt her but she never bore resentment and her eyes were always warm and loving when she glanced at him, her lips parted instinctively for his kiss when he drew her to him, and he could not doubt her happiness in their marriage.

Clifford would be pleased that things were working out so well. He had been a little dubious about the marriage, thinking of the differences of their ages, thinking of Judith's lack of experience and knowing that Mark was a man of the world, doubting that Mark could make his daughter happy.

Perhaps it would be a good idea to invite Clifford, his wife and the two children, down to the Lodge when they returned from Paris. They had not seen them since the wedding and Judith spoke frequently of her father. Surely in her own home, she would be able to forget her jealousy of Mary and make her welcome. Although Mark did not want children of his own and did not, as a rule, care for them in any case, he found Mary's two youngsters very appealing. He could stand them about the place for a few days, anyway—yes, it was a good idea and he would suggest it to Judith when she came home that night. It would be her first chance to entertain house guests since they were married and he was sure she would be glad of the opportunity to play hostess, especially to her own father. Clifford would have ample scope to realize her happiness in her marriage and to approve her choice of husband...

CHAPTER IV

Judith smiled at Mark over the rim of her tall glass. He lounged comfortably in a chair on the other side of the small round table, perfectly at ease, a cigarette dangling from his fingers, his drink on the table before him.

The bar lounge of the big hotel was busy but not crowded. The crowds would fill Paris later in the year when Spring had touched the city with colourful and lively fingers. Paris now was cold and wet and very much like the London they had left two days ago. They planned to stay for five days only but Mark promised his wife that they would return again in the summer.

She smiled at him now because she was happy and contented. She had packed for their brief stay in Paris with a light heart and a thrill of excitement—a few days abroad with her husband was an unexpected pleasure and she looked forward to being alone with him.

She leaned forward suddenly. 'Mark, do you realize that this is our first chance to be alone since we were married?' Her voice rose on a note of excitement. 'There's always someone around at the Lodge—the servants, Casey, the Mallows, the Ancells. We're never really alone.'

Mark grinned, gestured vaguely about him. 'You call this being alone?' He indicated the people standing at the bar, those entering the lounge at that moment, others who sat at similar small tables scattered about the room.

Judith nodded. 'We don't know a soul here!' she exclaimed, 'and that's a great relief!'

Mark glanced at his watch and then drained his glass. 'In a minute, Marcel will be with us for dinner,' he reminded her. 'He's one soul in Paris that we do know.'

'He's different,' Judith said quickly. 'He's a business associate...'

'And my friend!' Mark amended sharply.

'Yes ... but he isn't one of our set so his conversation isn't full of the people we know and the latest scandal about them!'

Mark grinned. 'I'm surprised that you can follow his conversation,' he said lightly.

Judith pouted a little. 'My French may not be *par excellence*,' she said quickly, 'but it isn't that bad!'

'Here is Marcel now!' Mark exclaimed and leaped to his feet as the Frenchman crossed the lounge to join them. The two men shook hands, then Marcel Toussaint bowed to Judith and greeted her courteously. He was of similar age to Mark and was in charge of the Paris gallery. The two men were good friends and Judith had taken an instant liking to Marcel. His brown eyes shone now with warm admiration for the chic blue ensemble she wore, the sleek golden chignon of her hair, the smooth curve of her cheek. A true

Frenchman, his eyes were eloquent and his ardent gaze brought the faintest of flushes to Judith's fair skin. He sat down between them and Mark ordered fresh drinks. They sat for some little time, talking of this and that. Mark had reserved a table for dinner at the hotel and it was planned that they should go on to a night-club later.

The cuisine of the hotel was excellent. Marcel was full of praises during the meal. He was good company with a lively sense of humour and kept the conversation turning from one subject to another with the ease of long practice.

Marcel decided upon the choice of night-club. It was a roadhouse on the outskirts of Paris and well worth driving twelve miles. A very popular rendezvous at the moment, he told them, with the best cabaret in Paris, an excellent orchestra, beautifully tended gardens which were completely enclosed in glass containing ornamental ponds, fountains, lawns, exquisite floral pieces, subdued lighting—a very romantic setting, he added, and he had not forgotten that his friend Mark and the lovely Judith were still but newly-wed!

His extravagant description brought a smile to Judith's eyes but she readily agreed to the Frenchman's choice, admitting to a curiosity about the place.

When they reached the club, they were greeted by a small, brisk man with a black pointed beard. He welcomed Marcel with open arms and assured him that it would be a simple matter to provide him and his friends with a table although the inner room was packed. With a flick of his fingers, he brought a tall, distinguished character to his side. A few phrases in his quick French and they were led into the large, dimly-lit room with the tables so close together that the room looked far more crowded than it actually was. At the far end was the raised dais occupied by the orchestra and a tiny square of dance-floor. An empty table was miraculously provided and Marcel busied himself with the wine list. Mark touched Judith's hand briefly.

'What do you think of it?' he murmured.

She looked about her at the walls with their decorative but daring murals. She smiled. 'It looks like a den of iniquity,' she replied briefly.

Marcel, whose English was excellent, heard her and glanced up from the wine list. 'Ah, but it is really a most respectable place, I assure you.' At that moment, the room was plunged into darkness. 'Do not worry,' Marcel added quickly. 'We have arrived just before the cabaret—it is not a raid, I promise you!'

An expectant hush fell on the room. Then one bright red spotlight shone upon the small square of polished wood that was the dance-floor. The light fell upon a woman—beautiful, slim, the white gown she wore turned to flame in the spotlight. She stood with head bowed until the applause died down—then lifting her head, she began to sing. Her voice was sultry, the song more than a little naughty and typically French, her approach to her act seductive and intriguing.

Mark leaned forward towards Marcel. 'Who is she?'

'Manon Linsé—the newest sensation of Paris. Delightful, is she not?'

The singer finished her song, flashing a laughing, provocative glance upon her audience, and then slipped away during a tumult of applause.

She was followed by a French comedian whose quips moved the two men to laughter. Judith found his quick French difficult to follow—and decided it was just as well, judging by his uproarious reception! The occasional remark she did catch brought a flush to her cheeks, much to Mark's amusement.

A team of dancer-acrobats came on next and they were followed by a brilliant juggler. The cabaret finished abruptly, the lights went up and the orchestra began to play dance-music.

Marcel turned to Judith. 'Will you dance with me? Mark, you do not mind?'

Mark shook his head. 'Not at all. Dancing isn't really much in my line. You go ahead, Judith.' He rose to his feet as Judith nodded and slipped her stole from her shoulders.

Mark sat watching them. The dance-floor was too small for much movement and too crowded to be comfortable yet Judith seemed to enjoy herself. She laughed up into Marcel's eyes and he was entertaining her with his easy conversation, his gay humour. When they returned to the table, Judith picked up her evening-bag and excused herself from them. Mark nodded then turned to Marcel with an open cigarette-case.

Judith made her way across the room to the powder-room. It was a matter of moments to powder her pretty nose, to brush back a few wisps of hair, to adjust the neckline of her dress. She returned to the smoky, crowded room, glanced across at their table. Mark and Marcel were engrossed in their conversation. As she moved to make her way towards them, someone touched her arm and she turned abruptly, surprised.

'Judith! What in the world are you doing here?'

Blue eyes smiled down at her. White teeth flashed in a bronzed, good-looking face. A face that brought swift memory flooding. A voice, deep, pleasant, vibrant, which stirred to life forgotten emotions. For a long moment, she just looked into his eyes and her present surroundings were non-existent. Then she pulled herself together and smiled a response, automatically, formally polite but distant.

'I'm sorry—should I know you?'

'Of course you should—and you do! Don't pull any tricks, my sweet and lovely Judith! What a wonderful surprise to find you here!'

She looked about her swiftly. Then almost furtively, at Mark who sat with his back to her and could not have witnessed this encounter.

She turned back to the man who still regarded her quizzically. 'Perry—I can't talk to you now. I thought I'd never see you again...' She broke off. Her thoughts and emotions were in turmoil. So many memories!

'Where are you staying?' he asked quickly, softly. 'I'll telephone you...'

'Hôtel le Grand,' she replied automatically. 'But you mustn't ring me,' she told him quickly. 'I'm married, Perry—my husband is sitting over there. I must go...'

He caught her arm and his grip hurt. 'I'd heard of your marriage,' he said and she heard the trace of pain in his voice. 'I must talk to you soon. I'll call you!' He released her arm, turned on his heel and walked back to his table.

Judith returned to her own table, striving for composure. Mark glanced up from the conversation, smiled, did not seem to notice her pallor, and returned to Marcel.

Judith sat toying with the glass that stood before her. She was very conscious that Perry's eyes were on her and she knew that if she turned to look at him she would meet accusation and pain in their depths. That she should meet him here! People said it was a small world—how right they were! It had been in Paris that they had first met. How long ago it all seemed—three years—three summers ago!

She had spent the summer with friends who rented an apartment in the city at the first sign of life, returning to their house in Cannes when the summer drew to an end. Judith had gone to finishing-school in Paris with Bar Gates-Hedley and they had become firm friends. It had been a wonderful summer with Paris at its loveliest, glorying in the sun. Perry lived in Paris. He was the son of a British diplomat working and living in the city and Perry himself was half-French. He had inherited his mother's Gallic charm but his father's fair hair and skin, the blue eyes and blond lashes. Tall, slim, handsome—it was not surprising that Judith had lost her heart to him very quickly. But it was no more than a summer madness and Judith quickly forgot her turbulent emotions when she returned to England at the beginning of autumn.

Arriving in Paris with Mark, she had known a slight thrill of nostalgia for those summer days, the happiness and zest for living that she and Perry had shared. Almost unconsciously, she had scanned the tree-lined avenues, the bustling markets, the familiar squares, hoping for a sight of the tall, slim boy she had once loved—briefly, it was true, but first love was never forgotten. The sight of a fair head, an inflection in a man's voice, a familiar name spoken by a passer-by—all these had stopped the beat of her heart for a swift moment. Yet she had not really expected to meet him—had not really wanted to see him again. Youthful adventures are best forgotten, she had told herself—and she was married to Mark whom she loved. But she could not deceive herself. She was glad that they had met and she could not help hoping that he would telephone her. There could be no harm in meeting him for an aperitif—for a nostalgic talk of old times—Mark would understand and consent. She would tell him later of her encounter with Perry...

They rose to leave a little later. Mark's eyes casually scanned the room and then he frowned slightly. He turned to Judith. 'That man over there seems to know you, my dear. He's been watching you for some time. Do you know him—or is he merely being insolent?'

Judith swallowed and hastily draped her stole about her shoulders, pretending to be engrossed in its folds. Annoyance was in Mark's voice and she said quickly, striving for nonchalance: 'I don't know him from Adam...'

'I think I'll have a word with him,' Mark began firmly. 'I object to the way he's staring at you!'

She pulled at his arm. 'Don't create a scene, Mark—I hate scenes. He doesn't mean any harm—perhaps he admires my gown—please, Mark!'

Surprised by her agitation, he allowed himself to be drawn away. He put a possessive arm about her waist and glared back at the insolent young man as they made their way from the room.

Marcel had acknowledged some friends in the club earlier and he decided to join them when Mark assured him that he and Judith were returning to the hotel rather than seeking fresh entertainment.

Judith sat beside Mark in the hired saloon car, her fingers twining restlessly. She regretted denying Perry but the deed was done now. It would have been easier and more creditable to admit that they had once been friends, taken Mark across to introduce him to Perry, and smooth the way for she and Perry to meet in the future. It was impossible now to tell Mark the truth—what explanation could she give for her first denial of Perry's existence? Mark would be instinctively suspicious of something that was perfectly innocent and above-board. Judith told herself firmly that her only reason for wanting to see Perry again, to talk with him, was because they had once shared a summer of happiness and gay friendship. She wanted to find out what he had been doing with his life during the last three years: she wanted to know if he had matured—but his Gallic blood had blessed him with early maturity. He must be twenty-five now, she told herself, calculating—were there other women in his life? Surely there must have been during the last three years! An icy finger touched her heart. But she could not expect him to have remained faithful to her memory, she chided herself. Indeed, she hoped he had not—for she was married to Mark now and Perry must realize that. There could be no point in raking up old emotions—but there was no reason why their friendship should not be renewed. Judith was strangely innocent in her thoughts...

Mark sensed her need of silence and he drove capably, quietly, back to the hotel. Perhaps she was tired—but their life had not been unduly exciting since their arrival in Paris. Mark's trip was mostly concerned with business although he found time to accompany Judith on any excursion. It was fortunate, he told himself, that this was not Judith's first visit to the great city, or he would be rushed off his feet on sight-seeing tours! She had told him of the summer in Paris a few years ago and mentioned that she would like to visit the friends she had stayed with—but they would probably be in Cannes at this time of the year. She was perfectly happy in renewing acquaintances with some of the best-loved places in Paris while he sat at conference with Marcel and the other members of the firm, or called on old friends and customers and connoisseurs of the art world.

Mark was in the bath when the telephone

rang the following morning. Judith's heart turned over then she hurried from the breakfast table to the instrument. A few moments delay and then she was connected by the operator to her caller.

'I wish to speak to Mrs Debenham...' Perry began.

'This is Mrs Debenham,' Judith replied rapidly, softly, her heart thumping. 'Is that you, Perry?'

'Good morning, my sweet. Where are we going to meet—and when? It's a fine day—no March wind and the sunshine is giving a touch of splendour to the Tuileries.'

'Is that where you are?' she asked eagerly.

He chuckled. 'Not at this hour, Judith— I'm as lazy as ever.' He paused. 'Are you alone?'

'At the moment,' she said. 'Mark is—Mark's dressing...'

'How very convenient!' he applauded. 'Tell me, my sweet, what shall I be?

111

Your dressmaker—an appointment with the hairdresser...?'

'Mark has an appointment this morning,' she interrupted. 'He doesn't keep check of my movements—he won't question me.'

'A complacent husband—typically English,' Perry mocked. 'If I had a beautiful wife, I should want to know where she spent every minute of her day—and night!'

'Look, Perry, I must go. Mark will be out in a minute...' Panic lurked in her voice.

'The Tuileries then—eleven o'clock?' His voice deepened. 'I can't wait to be with you, Judith.'

'Yes—yes. All right, Perry. Eleven o'clock.' She replaced the receiver in a panic as the dining-room door swung open and Mark came in. He glanced at Judith with interest as she stood guiltily by the telephone table.

'Who was that?' he asked casually.

'It—it was a friend of mine,' she stammered. 'I shall probably be out to lunch, Mark ... do you mind?'

He smiled. 'Of course not. But I thought your friends were out of Paris at the moment.' He sat down at the table and picked up the newspapers. It was of little real interest to him. His thoughts were mainly on a big business deal he hoped to bring off successfully that day.

'It was Bar,' she explained hastily. 'She heard I was in Paris. She motored up from Cannes yesterday. Perhaps she saw the news of our arrival in a newspaper...' The lies reeled from her tongue and she was horrified but it was too late to prevent them reaching his ears.

'That's nice,' he approved absently. 'I should like to meet this Bar of yours,' he added. 'Perhaps we could lunch together.'

'Oh no!' she said quickly, and then at his surprised look, 'it's so long since we met, darling. We shall probably talk nineteen to the dozen—all about old times and people you've never met. We'd bore you to death.'

He shrugged. 'Ask her to dine with us one evening, then,' he said casually. 'Marcel can make up the four.'

'Yes—yes, I'll do that,' she promised. She moved towards the bedroom.

'Have you had breakfast?' he called after her.

'I only wanted coffee,' she replied from the doorway. She didn't add that she had been too tremulous and excited to eat, that a sixth sense had told her that Perry would ring her that morning. She did not stop to analyse her pleasure that he had telephoned or her painful thrill of anticipation when she thought of their meeting in the Tuileries. She closed the bedroom door behind her. She was deceiving Mark. The thought upset her yet she could not go to him and explain her lies. Why should she have lied? If she could find no reason, surely Mark would find it even more difficult to understand her actions. Mark was no demanding jealous husband. Surely he would approve of her meeting with an old friend—so why was

114

she afraid to tell him about Perry? The answer eluded her and wearily she stripped out of her housecoat and padded into the bathroom to run the hot water.

Her heart thudded painfully as she waited for Perry. She knew exactly at what point in the Tuileries he meant them to meet—it was their old meeting-place of three years ago. As she stood, attracting the occasional glance of admiration or curiosity, the years seemed to slip away— and she was twenty years old, fair and lovely, suffering all the pain and heartache of first love. Until he came towards her with the familiar smile of welcome and joy suffused her—then it was that Judith realized with a start that she was now three years older, her love for Perry had long since died, and she was married to Mark Debenham.

But Perry gave her little time to think. He took her hands and lifted them, one after the other, to his lips. Then, with a hand under her arm, he led her towards the gates and out into the broad avenue. They walked over to a café. Though it was only late March, the sun was shining brightly if not warmly, and the proprietor had put out the small tables and brightly painted chairs. Several Parisians and visitors to Paris had decided to stroll in the Tuileries, despite the bleakness, and the proprietor was determined to attract custom to his café.

Perry ordered wine and then he leaned his elbows on the round table and gazed into Judith's face. They had barely exchanged a word since they had met.

Now he said slowly: 'I think you are even more beautiful, my sweet. Marriage or maturity? Which?'

Judith shrugged. 'You haven't changed at all, Perry,' she told him.

'I'm three years older,' he replied. 'A little wiser, one hopes—but who can tell? It perhaps isn't very wise to be here with you like this, Judith?'

She shook her head. 'Not wise—but I'm

116

glad I came, Perry. I couldn't see that we'd ever meet again—unless through Bar and I haven't seen her in such a long time.' She leaned forward eagerly and put her hand on his arm. 'How are you, Perry? Are you well—are you happy? You're not married or anything?'

His fingers closed over hers. He answered her last question. 'There's never been anyone but you, Judith.' His voice was low and serious.

In her surprise, the words slipped out: 'Not in three years!'

He gave an odd Gallic gesture. 'The odd affair or two—but no one who meant to me what you did, my sweet! I loved you—you knew that?'

She smiled into his eyes. 'I loved you, Perry—but it's a long time ago and emotions change with time.'

'Yes.' He sighed. 'Emotions change— and you fell in love again. Now you're a married woman—and if I took notice of my English conscience, I should leave you this moment and never seek you out again.' He smiled, his lips parting to show firm white teeth. 'But I've a French heart and a romantic nature—so we'll drink wine together and then I shall take you to lunch at Pére Andrés restaurant. We will snatch at these few brief days together, my sweet—and try to recapture the past.'

'No,' Judith said firmly. 'No, Perry—I can't do that. You mustn't encourage me to be deceitful—Mark trusts me...'

Perry squeezed her fingers. 'Of course he trusts you—and I'm not asking you to betray that trust. I'm only asking for a renewal of friendship, for a few hours of your company—where is there wrong in that?'

'I don't know,' Judith said helplessly. 'But I am sure I shouldn't see you again, Perry—this is Paris and people talk. If anyone saw me with you—and knew that I'm Mrs Mark Debenham—they'd jump to awful conclusions...'

'Nonsense!' he chided her. 'Paris is for

lovers in the Spring—who would imagine us to be lovers, sitting here on a bleak March morning, sipping wine, talking of this and that. Judith, my sweet, you have a vivid imagination.' He touched her cheek with a caressing hand. 'We were so happy—three years ago,' he added softly.

Her eyes shone suddenly. 'How wonderful it would be to re-live that summer, Perry. I don't think I've ever been so happy—or felt so young and carefree. I'll always adore Paris because of the months we spent together here.' She was suddenly eager. 'Tell me, do you still want to write, Perry? Are you working? Does your father still disapprove?'

'So many questions,' he laughingly replied. But he did his best to answer them and many others that she put to him.

The morning sped on wings and she was happy in his company. They lunched at the restaurant he had mentioned and Pére André welcomed Judith with open arms and a torrent of excitable French. It was an embarrassing moment when he stood back a little from her, turning to Perry, and said brightly: 'So the lovebirds were married, after all?'

Judith understood his words and she flushed, throwing an anxious glance at Perry, who brushed the remark aside adroitly and demanded the best meal in all Paris, prepared by Pére André himself.

At last reluctantly, Judith had to leave Perry and return to the hotel. He put her into a taxi and stood by the open door for a few moments.

'Tomorrow, *cherie?*' he asked softly.

She was doubtful for the briefest of moments. Then she nodded, smiling happily. 'Yes, if I can. Don't telephone me, Perry. I'll call you—is it the old address?'

He shook his head. 'No—I don't live with my parents any longer. I have taken a studio where I try to write.'

'Can I telephone you there?'

'No. I'll wait for you at the main entrance to the Louvre, Judith. Ten-thirty. If you have not arrived by eleven-thirty, I shall know that something prevents you from coming. Then I shall ring you.'

'I shall be there,' she promised him while it occurred to her that she must find some other excuse to give Mark—she could still use Bar for the time being. It flashed through her mind that she should get in touch with Bar and ask her help—ask her to come to Paris for a few days to meet Mark and renew their friendship.

He lifted her fingers to his lips. 'This has been a wonderful day,' he murmured. 'But too short.'

'Mark will be home by now,' she said. 'I have to get back to the hotel. Until tomorrow, Perry.'

He smiled ruefully. 'I must be patient—until tomorrow, my sweet.' He slammed the taxi door, gave instructions to the driver, and then stood on the kerb as the taxi shot away, looking after it for a few minutes. Judith turned on the slippery seat to wave a hand to him—then they turned a corner and Perry was lost to sight.

She entered the hotel suite, humming blithely—and stopped, feeling a start of guilt, as she came face to face with Mark.

'Hallo, there!' he exclaimed. He glanced at his watch. 'You certainly had plenty to talk about, my dear—your luncheon nearly stretched to tea!'

She laughed lightly. 'Bar is a great talker,' she said. She slipped out of her heavy coat, threw her bag and gloves on to the table. 'How was the conference?'

'Much the same as any other,' he replied. He offered her a cigarette which she refused. 'A great deal of discussion—and very little decision.' He paused and then crossed to the bell push. 'I thought we'd take in a show this evening, Judith—I'll send for the papers and we can find out what's on.' He glanced quickly at her. 'You aren't too tired?'

'Of course not. I think it's a good idea.'

He studied the glowing end of his cigarette. 'Do you think your friend Bar would care to go with us, Judith? Could you telephone her?'

Judith flashed him a swift, suspicious glance. Then she quickly improvised: 'Bar loves the theatre—but she has an engagement for tonight. She told me so—' she laughed. 'As it's a man, I'm sure she wouldn't care to break her date!'

'It was just a suggestion,' Mark said casually. 'I'm very interested in meeting Bar—I want to meet all your friends, Judith, my dear...'

CHAPTER V

Could Mark possibly suspect that Bar wasn't even in Paris? Lying in bed that night, Judith turned the thought over and over in her mind. He had passed several comments that evening which sounded casual and innocent enough—unless one had a guilty conscience. Judith rather resented being made to feel guilty. It was true that she was deceiving Mark—seeing Perry and telling lies about it was deceitful—but if he had been the type of man to whom one could talk of such things as past romances and the yearning to recapture the glamour of those days, then Judith would have told him. But she was sure that he would never understand or approve. Suddenly he had turned into a stranger—which was ridiculous, she chided herself. Paris had intoxicated her—Paris and Perry. It had been wonderful to be with him again—to listen to his deep and pleasant voice, to draw his laughter, to catch the eager light in his eyes and know that she was the one responsible for that light, to know the touch of his lips on her fingers, the pressure of his hand on her arm, to exchange memories and confidences and events which had happened to them both since they had been young and in love.

She was awake for some time and assumed that Mark slept in the other bed. His breathing was regular and even. Returning from the show, they had enjoyed a last drink and a cigarette. Then Judith had pretended to a weariness she did not feel so that she could slip between the cool sheets, bathed in the darkness, and let her thoughts return to Perry. Mark had come to bed some time later, undressing in the dark so he did not disturb her, bending over her bed to drop a brief, cool kiss on her forehead.

Judith was in the mood to resent that casual caress. He was such a cold man, she stormed to herself—cold and unfeeling against Perry's youthful, warm passion. There was passion in every glance that Perry gave her; subtle meaning in the tones of his voice, in the pressure of his fingers on hers; ardent longing behind every word, every gesture. But Mark! How often did he seek her embraces, how often did his kisses hold any real warmth? She was a young woman and the blood ran warm in her veins—was it surprising—no, would it be surprising if she should turn to another, a younger man for the passionate love-making that her husband denied her.

At this point, her hand flew to her mouth in horror. Her thoughts were running beserk! That she could even think such a thing—of being unfaithful to Mark. What spell had Paris and Perry cast upon her that the love which usually flowed through her whenever she thought of Mark seemed suddenly barren and worthless! She still loved him—nothing would ever alter that, she told herself fiercely. But had it already been changed, came the thought—had it already altered a little, in subtle manner and unknown to her, during their few weeks of marriage? It was possible—but Judith fought against the idea. She wanted to go on loving Mark because he had always seemed worthy of her love—no one else, not even Perry, could merit the amount of love and adoration which filled her heart. Mark was the only one who surpassed her ideals of the perfect husband—except for his coldness, his lack of love for her, and she hoped that one day she would win his heart.

Tears came to scald her cheeks. Silent tears—for she would not disturb Mark. If only he would love her just a little—so that she could find a real and lasting happiness in their marriage. If only she had not lied about Perry—now it would mean more lies for she could never tell Mark the truth. How disappointed he would be in her! He would assume her love to be very weak if she could find happiness in another man's company—but that wasn't the case at all. It was simply that her love found no response—and her lonely heart turned to the obvious admiration and affection of other men. Not that Mark could ever understand that—no man would, she assured herself. She rubbed the back of her hand across wet lashes...

It seemed incredible the next morning that she could possibly have slept. Yet she had done so—soundly and well, despite her troubled emotions. She stirred as Mark spoke her name and then she sat up to find him standing by her bed with a breakfast tray.

'You were tired last night,' he said. 'I thought you'd rather breakfast in bed.'

She leaned across to the slim gold watch which lay on the table between the beds. Horrified, she looked at the position of the tiny hands. It was almost ten—and in half an hour's time she should be at the

Louvre. Ignoring the tray, she thrust back her covers. 'I don't want breakfast, Mark,' she said, slipping into her gown. 'I've an appointment at ten-thirty—and I shall be very late unless I hurry.'

He frowned. 'You should have mentioned your appointment, Judith. I would have woken you earlier.'

'I'd forgotten all about it...' she called over her shoulder on the way to the bathroom.

'You've plenty of time,' he assured her. 'I'll drive you wherever you want to go.'

Her reply was lost in the sound of running water. He put the tray down and idly picked up the pile of letters which he had propped against the small cut-glass vase which held a rose. He ran through the pile. Two from England—one was in Clifford's handwriting, the other—he frowned slightly—was a pale-blue envelope with a Cannes postmark which had been forwarded on from the Lodge. He studied the angular, feminine handwriting—then shrugged and put the envelope with the others. Other letters were postmarked Paris—probably from hairdressing or dress-making salons in search of custom while the Debenhams were in France.

Judith ran quickly through her letters while she dressed. A little gasp escaped her when she came to the envelope from Cannes. Pausing in her dressing, she ripped open the letter and read the contents. Then she sat for a few minutes with the letter in her hand, frowning, almost forgetting that she had little time in which to get to the Louvre for her appointment with Perry.

Life played some funny tricks! Here was she, in Paris, rushing off to meet a mythical Bar who should be happily spending the winter in Cannes—and Bar had decided to make a trip to London and was probably in the great metropolis at this very moment. The irony of the situation forcibly struck Judith. So it would be impossible to ring Bar today and get her to travel up to Paris so she could dine with the Debenhams. If

Mark was suspicious at all, it would do nothing to allay his suspicions if Judith was unable to produce her friend Bar during the rest of their short stay in Paris...

Mark adjusted his tie and watched Judith in the mirror. 'Is anything wrong?' he asked, speaking casually.

'Wrong? Oh no!' she exclaimed sharply. She folded the pages, thrust them back into their envelope and threw the letter aside. Picking up her comb, she ran it through her blonde hair and hastily swept the tresses into the chignon. She applied last-minute make-up, conscious that the minutes were slipping by. But Perry had promised to wait an hour for her if necessary. Mark held the thick red winter coat while she slipped into it.

'Where is it you're going?' he asked idly. 'It might be in my direction.'

'It isn't,' she replied quickly. 'I don't want to take you out of your way, Mark—I'll get a taxi.'

'I've plenty of time,' he assured her.

'Please don't bother.' She spoke sharply, her voice tinged with panic. He raised his eyebrows and a flush stained her cheeks. She pulled herself together and said, more calmly: 'I'm going the other side of the river, Mark—it would be silly for you to drive me all that way. I can get a taxi...'

He shrugged. Then with a light laugh, he added: 'You're being very secretive about Bar—is she so attractive? Are you afraid I might fall for her?'

'All things are possible in Paris,' she returned lightly, gathering up gloves and handbag.

Mark said oddly: 'All things are possible of all men—and women, too.' With a change of tone, he added: 'Will you meet me for lunch?'

'Thank you—but Bar has arranged for us to lunch with some old friends.' She turned towards the door. 'I used to know them very well when I was in Paris three years ago. The Congrieves.'

Mark's eyes narrowed. 'Sir Audley

Congrieve—the British diplomat?'

'Yes, that right. Do you know them, Mark?'

'I know of them,' he replied. 'I've never actually met Sir Audley or his wife. Run along then, my dear—if you won't let me drive you to your appointment, then I have time for another coffee before I leave for mine.'

Excitement filled her because she was meeting Perry and relief flooded her because she had escaped Mark's courteous escort, she turned and blew him a kiss from the door of the suite. 'Bye, Mark,' she called and the door closed behind her.

Perry was waiting. Pacing up and down with a trace of impatience in his movements, he was a tall figure that quickly drew attention. His fair hair stirred in the breeze that had sprung up and he wore a heavy duffel coat against the cold and the damp. When he caught sight of Judith hurrying towards him, he hastily threw his cigarette into the gutter and turned to greet her.

'Perry, I'm sorry I'm late,' she stumbled eagerly. 'I wondered if you'd wait for me.'

'I told you I would wait.' There was a hint of reproach in his voice. He took her hand. 'Why, you're cold,' he said and his voice took on a note of tenderness. 'I suggest we have coffee now, darling—and discuss what you would like to do today.'

The fragrant and steaming coffee between them, his eyes smiled across at her and Judith felt contentment steal over her.

'I've parked my car nearby,' he told her. 'Shall we drive out to Versailles?'

She shivered slightly. 'It isn't really the right sort of weather, is it?'

He shrugged. 'I'm not in the mood for art galleries and such indoor entertainment...' He paused. 'But of course,' he added gallantly, 'if you wish to visit the Louvre...'

She stopped him with a quick gesture.

'We viewed it so many times, Perry—do you remember?' She flashed him a reminiscent smile. 'If you would like to go for a drive, then that's what I would like, too.'

They walked to his parked car, hands linked and their conversation was gay and youthful. A few minutes later, Judith sat beside him as they sped through the rues and avenues of Paris. She did not question the happiness that possessed her or stop to analyse her emotions at all. She was with Perry—the years between had faded—and they were recapturing the old *camaraderie*, the youthfulness and affection, awakening the old emotions and recklessly pushing aside all thought of the present.

They lunched at Versailles. Perry was restless. Versailles held no novelty for him, no excitement. He wanted to drive on further, leaving the memory of Paris and Judith's husband behind them. He did not have to say this but Judith sensed it in the urgency of his suggestion, in his eagerness, in the passionate light in his eyes. She mentally shrugged. Why should she hurry back to an empty hotel suite? Mark would be busy all day—he would probably lunch with Marcel and then return to the gallery for further discussion and decision. He had to pack such a lot of business into these few days. They were due to leave for London on Friday—and they could not postpone it because her father and Mary had duly accepted the invitation to spend a few days at the Lodge.

A propos of nothing but her thoughts, Judith said suddenly: 'I'm leaving Paris on Friday.'

Perry put out a hand to touch her fingers gently.

'So soon?' His voice was caress. 'We have so much to say to each other, *ma petite!* You cannot leave me yet.'

She sighed. 'I have to go, Perry.'

He leaned forward. They were alone in the small restaurant where they had enjoyed an excellent luncheon. He spoke softly. 'But you are reluctant to go? You have enjoyed these last few days—with me? It's been fun, my sweet, hasn't it?'

Their eyes met: deep-blue depths mingled with the lighter Saxon blue. She nodded softly. Tearing her eyes away, she said casually: 'I love Paris.'

He lifted her fingers to his lips, kissed them ardently, one by one. 'And me also—just a little, eh?' He smiled warmly, richly, leaned forward to touch her slightly-parted mouth with his lips. A small sigh escaped her. She was almost mesmerized by his nearness and by the confusion of emotion within her. His touch stirred her blood and drove all thoughts of Mark from her mind.

'Perhaps,' she whispered softly.

He was suddenly strong, determined, his eyes narrowed. 'Of course you love me, Judith. This marriage of yours is a mistake. You and your husband can have nothing in common. Why—' he sneered slightly—'he hasn't even the sense to love you!'

She was amazed, embarrassed at the

note of truth and a little chagrined. 'Perry!' she stammered. 'Why do you say that?'

He shrugged. The gesture was very Gallic. 'I think I know your character very well, my sweet. You would not have married this man Debenham unless you thought yourself in love with him. Also, with your strong English principle, you would never have agreed to meet me again if he returned your love.' He smiled slowly. 'Only a lonely woman—a frustrated woman—a woman whose love is not returned—seeks admiration from another man and is willing to encourage the attentions she is offered.'

She raised her chin proudly. 'Perry, only the fact of the friendship we once shared induces me to forgive you such impertinence!'

'Friendship!' he exclaimed. 'We were in love—I wanted to marry you. I shall never understand why you wrote in the autumn to say that our affair was ended.'

'It was ended, Perry.' She spoke levelly.

'I loved you—but not enough to marry you. It was nothing but a summer madness...'

'On your part!' he flashed. 'But what of my emotions? What of the love I bore you? I still love you, Judith!'

She shook her head. 'You mustn't say such things to me, Perry. Not now—and never again!'

'Because you have a husband!' The sneer was more pronounced. 'A man who does not value the treasure in his possession. He prefers to scour Paris for art treasures of great value, neglecting his beautiful and valuable wife!' He rose to his feet and paced the room, smoking, visibly agitated. 'Tell me, Judith—and once again forgive my impertinence!—how often does your husband speak of his love for you? How often does he hold you with desire in his heart? Is he an ardent and eager lover? I think not! If he were, you would never look to me to provide the warmth and affection which you lack in your marriage.'

All colour had drained from Judith's

face. She had listened to him without protest and she was filled with shame that she had ever agreed to an assignation with him in the first place. Shame that she had put herself in a position where Perry could say such things to her! Shame that she allowed him to besmirch her husband's name and character.

Lacking a reply to his tirade, Perry stopped pacing up and down and glanced at her white face and the stricken eyes. Immediately he regretted his words.

'Judith, I'm sorry. Will you forgive me?' His voice was gentle now, and appealing. 'I had no right to say such things to you. Believe me, I'm sorry!' He bent his head and brushed the top of her golden head with his lips. 'I love you so much,' he murmured against her hair. 'I can't bear to think that you belong to another man. I'm riddled with jealousy, my sweet...'

She lifted her head and smiled reluctantly.

'That reckless tongue of yours,' she chided him.

He gestured helplessly with his hands. 'It's always been my worst enemy,' he admitted. He threw himself down in the chair beside her. 'Am I forgiven? Say you forgive me, *ma petite!*'

'I forgive you,' she said obediently but with little warmth. His eyes narrowed but he had to accept her words at face value.

'Let's get out of this depressing place!' he exclaimed sharply. '*Garcon! L'Addition, s'il vous plâit!*'

Once more seated in the car, Perry turned to Judith. 'Where shall we go?'

She looked a little dubious. Glancing at her watch, she said: 'Surely we should return to the city—we really haven't time to go on.'

'Nonsense!' he exclaimed. 'There's an enchanting little village with a very old church not more than ten miles from here. I discovered it last summer and it's a gem of a place—even in bleak March,' he added with a grin. 'I know you'll love it, Judith. I promise to put my foot down hard on the accelerator—and we'll still be back in town by evening.'

Her protests swept aside by his enthusiasm, she agreed to the venture. They bowled along the country lanes with more speed than care but Perry was such a confident and capable driver that she felt no fear. He narrowly missed an elderly Frenchman riding an ancient bicycle out of a side turning but the wind carried away the spate of French obscenity which followed them. Perry grinned. 'That was a narrow shave for Pierre,' he said blithely, swinging the wheel hard to avoid a sheep that had strayed on to the road. 'Thank goodness his comrades weren't fool enough to follow their leader,' he said easily. 'I can avoid one but a flock would drive me into the ditch.' He glanced at Judith. 'All right?' he asked. 'Enjoying the ride?'

Strangely, she was. Mark was always a careful driver, very capable on the roads but never taking an unnecessary risk. Speed thrilled her and she knew a little of Perry's own recklessness as they raced up and down hills, round bends, over badly-surfaced country roads in search of the tiny village.

'We're nearly there,' Perry assured her. 'When we turn this corner, you should be able to see the spire of the church—be sure to look out for it. I'll slow down a little...'

It was said, after, that only the fact of his removing his foot from the accelerator at that precise moment saved their lives. Rounding the corner at a steady amble came a donkey and a cart, the driver huddled under a thick blanket to keep off the drizzling rain and half asleep from the rhythmic movement of his conveyance. Perry saw the cart and swerved violently. They hurtled into the ditch and neither knew more until they recovered consciousness.

Judith stirred, vaguely conscious that her head was throbbing painfully. She opened her eyes for a moment and saw the white-robed figure who sat beside the bed, her fingers moving over the rosary beads, her lips moving soundlessly. Judith closed her eyes again. A cool, damp cloth touched her forehead lightly and a kindly voice spoke to her in French.

Judith opened her eyes and looked into the placid face of the woman who bent over her. Full consciousness came back to her suddenly and she demanded: 'Perry? Is he all right?'

She spoke in English.

'Perree? The young man—*votre mari?* He is well—*dormez-vous, mon enfant!*'

Judith struggled to a sitting position. A sharp stab of pain flashed through her head but she ignored this.

'Where is he?'

The nun patted her shoulder gently. 'He sleeps.'

Judith was clad in a linen gown and her hair had been loosened and fell about her shoulders. Her jewellery had been removed and she glanced at her wrist where her watch should rest. 'What time is it?' she demanded. 'I must get back to Paris—Mark doesn't know where I am!'

The nun looked a little bewildered. It was obvious that her English was not good enough to comprehend Judith's rapid remarks. Judith did not feel capable of translating her anxiety about Mark into the woman's own language. She threw back the covers and struggled to her feet. The nun laid a restraining hand on her shoulder.

'*Non, non, ma petite! Le docteur*—' She broke off as the door opened and turned a grateful face to the nun who entered. She burst into a rapid flow of French.

The second nun was older yet her face was unlined and serene. She came over to the bed and smiled down at Judith with innate kindness. Her hands were clasped comfortably at her waist.

'How do you feel, Madame Congrieve?'

'Oh, you speak English!' exclaimed Judith, in her relief ignoring the title.

'A little. Sister Marie understands—but

she finds it difficult to sort out her vocabulary when she is excited. How is your head?'

Judith put up a hand to brush back her hair. 'It aches—but not much. I'm perfectly all right, really.'

'Do you remember what happened?'

Judith shrugged—then winced as her head throbbed with the gesture. 'We had an accident in the car, I think. Perry took a corner too fast—and there was a horse and cart.' She glanced quickly up at the nun. 'Did we hit it?'

The Mother Superior shook her head soothingly. 'No, no. The donkey was untouched and Gaston Hulé is only shaken up.' She smiled. 'It will give him a story to tell for weeks to come.' She added: 'I think you should lie down again, *ma petite*. The doctor left strict orders that you must rest until morning when he will visit you again.'

'But I have to get back to Paris,' Judith protested. 'My husband—he will be so

146

anxious about me.'

'Your husband is in the next room,' Mother Superior assured her. 'He has not yet come round from the accident. But he will be all right,' she hastily added. 'The doctor says you both had a very lucky escape—your husband is only bruised and suffering from a little concussion.'

'But he isn't my husband,' Judith said anxiously. 'That's why I have to get to Paris. My husband doesn't know where I am.'

A faint look of disapproval touched the eyes of the Mother Superior. With a glance at the attendant nun, she said slowly: 'That is a great pity, Madame. We naturally assumed, as you were a married woman, that you were travelling with your husband.'

Judith flushed. To these dedicated women, so closely confined to the church, their lives so narrow and good, it must seem wicked and terrible that she should be deceiving her husband and careering

147

about the French countryside with a reckless young devil like Perry Congrieve. They must have found identity papers on him, she thought, a little confusedly—and remembered that she had no identification in her handbag, not even her passport, which was in Mark's care. A slight shudder passed through her. If she had been killed ... she might have been buried in the churchyard of the tiny old church which had so thrilled Perry with only a simple cross to mark her grave—a simple cross without a name.

She drew herself up proudly. 'My name is Judith Debenham—Mrs Mark Debenham. Is there any way I can contact my husband? He is staying at the Hôtel le Grand...'

Mother Superior shook her head. 'It is one o'clock in the morning, Madame,' she said slowly. 'There is no way of contacting him at this late hour.' She paused. 'Monsieur le Docteur will be here early this morning. He is hopeful that there will be no sign of concussion to retard your recovery. I expect you will be able to return to the city during the day.'

Judith ran her fingers through her hair.

'Mark will be frantic,' she said, almost to herself.

Mark had returned to the hotel for lunch and spent his afternoon in the suite, writing letters, reading articles in several French magazines, and waiting for Judith to return. He had promised a charming French woman, whom he had met that morning and with whom he had bargained for a priceless oil painting, that he would bring his wife to her home that afternoon for tea.

Time seemed to pass slowly and he frequently glanced at the elegant clock on the mantelpiece, frowning, wondering what on earth Judith was doing in Paris on such a cold and miserable day.

She had not returned by the time they were due at Madame Descartier's house. Reluctantly, angrily, Mark telephoned that good lady and made his apologies, explaining that his wife had developed *migraine* and had been advised rest. Madame Descartier was regretful and charming—and insisted that they should lunch with her on the morrow if Madame Debenham had recovered.

Mark was not anxious but he was very angry when Judith had not returned by the time he went down to the restaurant for dinner. Surely she could not have gone out to dinner with her girl-friend in the daytime clothes she had been wearing that morning? Mark shrugged. It was most unlike Judith—but then, she had been acting strangely during their stay in Paris.

During the meal, it occurred to him that she might have been invited to dine with the people they had lunched with. Or at least they might have some conception of her whereabouts. He racked his brains to remember the name—and it came to him in a flash. Congrieve! The diplomat. A telephone was brought to him

150

and a directory. In a few minutes time, he was connected to the number and speaking to Sir Audley Congrieve. That excellent personage was a little puzzled by the call—particularly as he had not seen Judith since she was in Paris three years ago and had no idea that she was now married and visiting France. He was even more astonished that Bar Gates-Hedley was supposedly in Paris and a guest at his house for lunch that very day.

'My dear Debenham, I was in to lunch—and my wife and I ate alone. My son was out somewhere. We had no guests. We know Barbara, of course—but she's in Cannes at the moment with her parents. To my knowledge, that is! I'm afraid I can't help you, sir.'

'I'm sorry to have bothered you, Sir Audley—but I'm sure my wife gave me your name when she mentioned her lunch appointment.'

'Perhaps she did, Debenham—perhaps she did! But she certainly didn't turn up here for lunch—and as far as I know, she wasn't an invited guest. My wife might know—I'll ask her if she invited Judith here...'

'It doesn't matter,' Mark said quickly. 'I dare say I misunderstood Judith's remark. Thank you very much, Sir Audley.'

He hung up, thoughtful. It was obvious what Sir Audley Congrieve had been thinking—but he was too good a diplomat and too courteous a gentleman to reveal his thoughts. Now, Mark began to think along the same lines. If Bar wasn't even in Paris, who the devil was Judith spending her days with? And where the devil was she at this very moment?

CHAPTER VI

The doctor finished his examination and indicated to Judith that she might dress.

'You were very lucky, Madame,' he told her. 'A few bruises and one or two cuts.' He gave a Gallic shrug. 'In a week you will forget that you were ever in a car accident. No sign of concussion fortunately.' He spoke English very well with only a faint trace of accent. 'Your husband too—a fractured rib which will heal quickly.'

Judith did not bother to correct him. Her only thought was to get back to Paris and Mark. She belted her dress, saying: 'Then there isn't any reason why we should stay here any longer?'

'Not at all.' He frowned slightly. 'You will not, of course, be able to use the car. It will need repair and I have suggested to your husband that he should arrange for its collection later. There is an excellent train service into Paris—at Versailles there is a garage which will hire you a car, if you prefer.'

Judith smiled, a little wanly. 'Thank you very much. You've been most helpful.'

'I would advise that you visit your own doctor in Paris and ask him for a mild sedative, Madame. It is possible that you will sleep badly for a few days—it must have been a shock.' He smiled.

Judith nodded. 'Certainly it was.'

He packed his instruments away. Then he held out his hand. 'Good-bye, Madame Congrieve.'

When he had gone, Judith wondered about the man's fee—but surely Perry would have seen to that. He had been very kind and reassuring. There was a gentle tap at the door and Perry entered. He hurried over to her.

'Are you really all right?' he asked anxiously.

154

She met his eyes coolly. 'No broken bones—no thanks to you, Perry.'

His smile faded. *'Mon Dieu!'* he exclaimed angrily. 'It was something that could happen to anyone—you cannot be angry with me, Judith!'

She ignored his words. 'How do you suggest we get back to the city?'

He shrugged. 'I have telephoned for a car. It will be here in half an hour.'

'Are you driving?' she asked.

He flushed slightly and walked towards the narrow window of the cell-like room. 'No,' he replied curtly. 'A chauffeur has also been hired. You will be perfectly safe...' There was a faint suggestion of a sneer behind the words.

Suddenly Judith exclaimed: 'You telephoned! Where is there a telephone?—I could ring Mark and explain.'

He turned and looked at her. 'You're very anxious about your husband. Do you really care for him, Judith?'

She nodded. 'Of course I do. I thought

you understood how I feel about him.'

A faint smile twisted his lips. 'You haven't made it very obvious, my sweet.' He sighed. 'Why the devil did we have to run into each other again? I've fallen in love with you all over again—and it's as hopeless now as it was three years ago.' There was a sadness behind his blue eyes which touched Judith's heart. She went over to him eagerly.

'Perry, I'm sorry!' She gave a bitter little laugh. 'If it's any good saying that! I didn't want to awaken old emotions, really—I never meant to hurt you.' She ran a hand over her hair in distress. 'What a fool I've been—trying to relive nostalgic memories. One just isn't meant to turn back the pages, I know that now.'

He put a cigarette between his lips, took a lighter from his pocket and inhaled deeply. Then he said, philosophically, 'Oh well, we've had some fun this week, *cherie*—and I'll always remember our days together. But now—' he gestured with his hands helplessly—'ring down the curtain! *Finis!*'

He accompanied Judith to the local inn and she telephoned to Paris. Waiting to be put through to Mark, the nerves in her stomach tightened and she hunted feverishly for the right words. To her astonishment, the operator informed her that Monsieur Debenham had left the hotel with the message that he would be at the gallery in the Rue de la Paix if he were wanted. Judith thanked the operator and put through a second call to the gallery. Perry tapped impatiently on the window of the booth. Judith opened the door.

'The car is here!' he told her. 'Are you going to be long? Can't you get through to Paris?'

'He wasn't at the hotel,' she replied shortly. She turned back to the telephone. 'Hallo!'

She finally heard Mark's voice and her heart stopped for a moment. He sounded cold and grim.

'Mark—it's Judith!' she stumbled.

'Where are you?' he asked curtly.

'Not far from Versailles,' she replied quickly. 'I'm just coming back to Paris—Mark, are you there? Mark, I want to explain...'

'Explanations can wait,' he cut her short.

'But you don't understand,' she began.

'I understand one thing very clearly,' he told her coldly. 'Your friend Bar hasn't been in Paris for months. I'm sorry that you found it necessary to lie to me about your movements.'

She was silent for a brief moment, her heart sinking. 'Are you very angry?' she asked him quietly at last.

She heard him draw in his breath sharply.

'I'm extremely disappointed in you,' was the curt reply. 'But I haven't time to talk to you now, Judith. I'm very busy. I shall be back at the hotel for lunch...' He added mockingly, 'I hope to find you at home!' Then he hung up.

Judith looked at the receiver she held. Then she replaced it slowly on its cradle, feeling sick at heart.

They were silent for most of the journey back to the city. Their chauffeur sat in front, whistling cheerfully and interminably. His driving was far from good but they arrived back in Paris safely, much to Judith's amazement. Perry leaned forward to give the man the address of the hotel.

With a screech of brakes, they pulled up at the entrance and then Perry turned to the pale, unhappy girl beside him. He took her hand and squeezed it. 'Well, Judith—is this *au 'voir?*'

She nodded slowly. 'Yes, Perry. I've deceived Mark long enough.'

'I shall never see you again?' He sounded despondent.

Judith shrugged. At the moment it was a matter of indifference to her. 'Who knows, Perry?' Her voice was hard.

He paused a moment. Then he said: 'I

shall be in London later this year. May I get in touch with you?'

She shook her head. 'I don't think that's a good idea...'

He interrupted her. 'I must see you again. Surely you will meet me for lunch—your husband could not object to that. We're old friends, aren't we?'

Judith sighed and glanced at the hotel entrance. 'I must go, Perry.'

'Not until you say yes!' he exclaimed.

'Very well,' she conceded ungraciously. 'We're on the telephone—ring me when you get to London and we'll arrange a meeting.'

He put an arm about her and drew her close. She struggled, resisting him. His lips came down on hers with swift, ardent pressure—and then he released her abruptly.

'Mark has so much,' he said softly. 'One kiss from your lips can easily be spared...' He leaned across and opened the car door. Judith hurried out of the car and left him without a backward glance. The commissionaire saluted her and pushed open the heavy swing doors of the hotel entrance. There was a flicker of amusement in his dark eyes and Judith was conscious that he had observed the little incident in the car.

She hurried to the desk and asked if her husband had returned. The clerk smiled and nodded. Monsieur Debenhan was in his suite.

Mark was standing by the window, looking down on the pavement below. He had seen the car arrive, noted Judith's hasty exit and caught a glimpse of the man who leaned forward to close the door of the car. His lips had tightened. He waited by the window, his expression grim. When Judith came into the suite, he did not turn to look at her. She paused by the door, looking at his broad back which seemed to express anger and coldness. For a long moment, neither of them made any movement or sound. Then Judith moved forward into the room, stripping off her gloves, trying to appear more composed than she felt.

'So you're back.' He spoke first, breaking the silence. She was shocked by his tone of voice, by the icy anger behind his words. He swung round and looked at her. She stepped back a little at the contempt in his cold grey eyes. He moved over to the table and poured a drink. Judith watched him.

She said slowly: 'Why are you so angry, Mark? Surely you should hear my explanation before deciding whether to be angry or not?'

He raised his eyebrows. 'Very well. Let me hear your story,' he sneered. 'You've had plenty of time to prepare it. I wonder if it will be as convincing as those about your friend Bar.'

Judith flushed. Proudly she walked towards the bedroom, slipping out of her heavy coat. 'My explanation can wait until you're in a better frame of mind, Mark. At the moment, I doubt if you'd believe a word of it.'

He drained the fiery whisky. 'I doubt if you're capable of telling the truth,' he retorted.

She spun round. 'That's a terrible thing to say to me!' she accused him.

He reached her side in a few strides and took her arm in a painful grip. 'You've lied to me consistently since we've been in Paris,' he said grimly. 'Can you deny that?'

Her eyes dropped beneath the accusation in his gaze. She tried to wrench her arm from his steely fingers. 'Mark, you're hurting me,' she said quickly. He released her, as she had been sure he would. Mark was no barbarian. He had always been courteous and kindly. Anger, such as that which possessed him now, and violence, seemed alien to his nature. With an effort, he recovered his temper. He moved back to the table and poured another drink, his hands trembling very slightly.

'Go and take your things off,' he said

evenly. 'I'll order lunch to be served up here. When we've eaten we'll talk things over.'

Carefully, Judith said: 'It won't take a minute to explain now, Mark.'

'After lunch,' he said firmly and picked up the telephone.

She ate very little. Mark also toyed with his food, though insisting that Judith should make a better meal. Apart from the slight coldness, he was attentive and polite. A deferential waiter was continually in the background so they talked seldom and only of banalities. Mark told her of their invitations to the Descartiers home and how regretful he was that both had been cancelled. He had telephoned Madame Descartier again that morning to apologize and explain that they would be unable to join her for lunch. He spoke of the painting she possessed and refused to part with. He mentioned the successful deal that he and Marcel had achieved that morning. Judith returned polite, noncommittal replies while her heart ached and her mind searched for the right words to heal the breach which seemed to make them strangers.

At last the interminable meal was over and the waiter deftly and swiftly cleared away the traces and bowed himself from the room, well pleased with the substantial tip that Mark had pressed into his hand.

Mark drew a comfortable armchair up to the fire and sat down, crossing his legs, and helping himself to a cigarette from his case. Judith wandered aimlessly about the room, nervous and restless. He watched her for a few moments, then indicated the chair opposite him.

'Sit down, Judith.'

Obediently, she came to the fireplace and sat down. Her fingers played absently with a small ornament she had picked up from the nearby small table. Mark leaned forward and removed it from her hands. She looked at him, biting her lip.

'You look like a naughty schoolgirl,' he

said with a lightness he did not feel. 'Relax, for heaven's sake!'

'How can I relax while you look at me with such accusing eyes?' she flashed at him sharply.

'Are they accusing? I'm sorry.'

'Why don't you ask me the questions that are seething through your brain?' she demanded. 'Why keep me in suspense?'

'I'm in no hurry to hear a pack of lies,' he told her curtly. 'But I suppose you'll tell me them, eventually—so, Judith, I'm waiting to hear your version of your actions.'

She twisted her rings on the left hand. 'I've done nothing wrong,' she began slowly. 'I admit I lied to you about Bar. She isn't in Paris. She's in London—but I didn't know that...'

'You were meeting a man,' he said wearily. 'I know that. So you fobbed me off with stories about a girl-friend.'

She stared at him in astonishment. 'You knew I was with a man?'

'Yes.'

'No wonder you're angry,' she said quickly. 'But don't jump to conclusions, Mark. He doesn't mean anything to me—I used to know him years ago—he's an old friend...'

'He doesn't mean anything to you,' he repeated. 'Yet you spent the night with him.' He lifted his eyes briefly to the ceiling. 'You must be completely without morals, Judith. If you were in love with the man, I could understand it...'

'That's how it sounds,' she said quickly. 'But we weren't together—I mean...' She broke off. How feeble it would sound if he were determined to believe ill of her. Pride suddenly swept through her. Why should she defend herself to him if he wanted to believe her capable of adultery? She raised her head arrogantly and her eyes were hard. 'Very well. So I spent the night with him. What are you going to do?'

He ignored her question. 'I must have neglected you shamefully for you to turn to another man a brief few weeks after marrying me. Unless, of course, I've been utterly mistaken in the woman I made my wife.' His eyes narrowed. 'I trust this is the first time you've been unfaithful to me? Casey...?' He broke off as pain swept through him. It was not easy for him to remain cool and composed, to keep his voice even while his thoughts were of Judith and another man, to hide the inner torment and disappointment and jealousy which possessed him.

Judith shook her head. 'You can think that Casey and I...?' She was dismayed. She could not believe that Mark could be so undisturbed, so complacent, if he really thought that she had been unfaithful. She bowed her head over her hands. So he was really incapable of affection, devoid of all love for her, thinking only of his pride and his name.

'I can believe anything of you now,' he replied. 'But somehow I don't think Casey would betray me. Who is this "old friend" of yours? What is his name?'

She raised her head. 'What are you going to do?' Surely he was not considering divorce, after all he had said on the subject. Fear gripped her. He must not divorce her. She couldn't live without him. She had had so little time with him, so little happiness.

'What is the man's name?' he repeated.

Judith leaned forward, her deep-blue eyes dark with pain, tremendous appeal in their depths. 'Please don't divorce me, Mark,' she said tremulously. It did not occur to her that he lacked the necessary evidence. She forgot that anyone seeking such evidence was bound to know the truth from the good nuns and the doctor.

'Don't be stupid!' he said sharply. 'Such an idea hadn't even occurred to me. If it did, I should certainly dismiss it.' He threw his cigarette into the fire. 'A fine thing—Mark Debenham divorcing his wife after five weeks of marriage! My God! The newspapers would give their eye-teeth for

169

such a story. Do you think I'm a fool!'

She regarded him oddly. 'That's your only reason? Fear of public opinion?'

'No. I disapprove of divorce. You know that very well, Judith. I've made my views very clear to you.' His mouth tightened. 'Perhaps that's why you weren't afraid to deceive me so openly—why you thought yourself safe in driving up to this hotel in a car with your lover!'

'He isn't my lover!' she snapped sharply.

He inclined his head. 'Forgive me,' he said with bitter sarcasm. 'For the moment, I forgot that love wasn't your motive.'

Judith clenched her hands so tightly that the long finger-nails cut her palms. 'Whatever I say now, Mark,' she said quietly, 'you wouldn't believe me, would you? If I denied your accusation,' she could not bring herself to mention the unpleasant word with all its implications, 'you would think I lied to you.'

His eyes met hers coolly. 'I'm afraid I would.'

She spread her hands in a helpless gesture. 'Have you ever had cause to think me a liar until now, Mark?'

He thought for a moment. Then he said: 'Shall we say that I've never caught you out in a lie before?'

How easy it would be to give him the truth and insist that he check her story. But her pride stopped her from doing so. Her heart was full of pain and desperate misery. He obviously wanted to think her a liar, wanted to think she could be unfaithful to the vows of her marriage. She could not understand why he could not bring an open mind to the incident.

Judith was blind to the fact that Mark had been so bitterly hurt by her actions, so disappointed in the woman he had thought to be good, sweet and loyal, that he knew a primitive, savage desire to hurt in return, to make her suffer a little as he had suffered during the hours of fear and anxiety, waiting all night for her return, unable to concentrate on anything

171

but the mysterious absence of his wife. To see her drive brazenly up to the hotel entrance with another man had been the last straw. He had realized in that moment how mistaken he was in her character, in her goodness, in her loyalty. Because he was not a man easily given to emotion, the shock of her treachery drove deep into his heart and brain. White rage seized him now as he thought of the man and he knew the primitive lust for revenge.

Once again, he asked: 'What is the man's name?'

Judith shook her head. 'I don't intend to tell you, Mark.'

He sneered. 'Misguided loyalty, my dear Judith. Well, it's of little interest to me. Are you afraid I should demand satisfaction from him?' He laughed lightly. 'Despite my appearance, I'm a physical coward.'

Judith rose to her feet. She was trembling and her head throbbed dully. She moved towards the bedroom. Mark put out a hand and caught her arm as she passed him. She stopped and looked down at him, startled.

'Shall I tell you why I would never divorce you?' he asked softly. With a swift movement, he rose and towered above her, looking down into her lovely face, which bore faint traces of strain. 'You're beautiful, Judith—very beautiful—and I'm a collector of beautiful things. I never part with any of my possessions—and you're a priceless possession.'

Pride slipped away from her, Judith put her arms around him and strained her slight body against his hard chest. 'Mark,' she whispered, 'Mark, don't be like this. Don't be hard and angry.' She pressed her mouth against the tiny pulse which throbbed in his throat. 'I love you, Mark,' she told him tremulously, sincerely, almost desperately.

He stood passive, unmoved by her appeal. Then he put her away from him firmly. She looked up at him, stricken, disbelieving. His eyes were contemptuous.

'You're inhuman!' she accused him tear-fully.

'No, I'm not inhuman,' he replied levelly. 'I merely find it rather distasteful that you should come to me from the arms of another man.'

For reply, she raised her hand and dealt him a sharp blow on the cheek. It was impulsive and rash and immediately regretted. Mark turned very white, the marks of her fingers red against the skin. His eyes were like steel and Judith stepped back involuntarily. He turned on his heel and walked to the window, where he stood for some time, motionless. Judith caught her lower lip between her teeth. She was shocked that she should lose complete control of herself and she knew that Mark would never forgive her that blow. Although she would forgive him his cruel words and his hurtful doubt of her, in time, because she loved him.

'Mark.' She spoke his name tentatively.

'Yes.' He did not turn round. The word

was curt and the ice cut her heart. Her lashes were wet and her throat ached with tears. But tears were useless. They would not wash away the breach which yawned even wider between them now.

'It isn't true,' she said dully. 'Last night...'

'I don't wish to discuss it any further.' He cut across her words firmly. 'You'd better go and pack. We're leaving Paris tonight.'

'But—our reservations are for Friday,' she reminded him, stunned.

'There are sometimes cancellations,' he said shortly. 'My business is completed—there's nothing to keep us in Paris.' Now he did turn round and the weals on his cheek still flamed, so hard had been the impact of her hand. 'Or is there any reason why you wish to stay?'

'No,' she said quickly. Her eyes dwelt on his cheek and she was filled with fresh shame. 'I'm sorry we came in the first place—it was a mistake.'

175

He spoke with grimness. 'Mistakes are sometimes unavoidable—but one learns not to repeat them!'

The airline officials were willing to oblige such a famous person as Mark Debenham and supplied him with two seats on the eight o'clock departure for London. They left Orly Airport on time and Judith leaned back in her seat and closed her eyes. It was a relief to leave Paris behind—Paris and Perry and all the complications they had brought. But the complications went with them for Mark's grim expression had scarcely changed. She stole a look at her husband's face through long lashes. The weals had faded from his cheek but they would leave a bruise on his heart and mind for a long time. Judith was still numb with despair and sadness. She was entirely to blame for the situation but knowing her own guilt did nothing to ease the ache in her heart.

It was late when they reached the Lodge.

A startled Alexander opened the front door to them.

'We didn't expect you, sir!' he exclaimed.

'Sorry.' Mark was curt. 'I tried to telephone from the airport but there's some trouble on the line.'

Sarah came bustling from the direction of the kitchen. 'Oh, my goodness!' she declared. 'The beds aren't even ready for you, sir.'

Mark gestured aside such unimportant details.

'We'll have coffee and sandwiches in the lounge, please, Sarah,' he said wearily. 'Is Mr Casey in?'

'He's gone away for a few days, sir,' Alexander replied. 'He was very restless after you left.'

Mark nodded and threw open the door of the lounge. He turned to Judith and helped her out of the fur coat she wore. She shivered slightly in the cold hall. At the sound of his master's voice, Digger barked in excited frenzy from the kitchen quarters. Mark went into the lounge and bent down to the fireplace. He put a light to it from his lighter. Then he glanced up at Judith. 'Damn nuisance that I couldn't get through,' he said. 'Alexander would have had this fire alight, hot coffee ready, and our rooms prepared.'

'The royal welcome, in fact,' she said, trying to speak lightly.

The logs were dry and quickly caught fire. By the time Alexander arrived with the coffee and sandwiches, the logs were blazing merrily. Digger had taken advantage of the open baize door which led to the kitchen to rush in search of his master. He leapt upon Mark joyfully, his pink tongue greeting him wetly, his tail declaring a welcome. Judith watched Mark's swift relaxation, the affection which he showered on the dog, the expression on Mark's face as he talked to Digger light-heartedly. The pain was almost unbearable and she turned away. How little affection he showed her and how much he had in his heart for Digger.

Mark glanced up and something in her face must have betrayed her thoughts. He said cruelly: 'He's a faithful animal—loyal to the core—and I know he means his declaration of love.'

She blanched at his words. Waves of pain swept over her and her senses swam. She swayed blindly and put a hand out to steady herself. Mark rose and looked at her white face, frowning a little. Then he said: 'Sit down, Judith.' He put a gentle hand on her shoulder and guided her to a chair. 'The journey has tired you,' he said. The kindness in his voice was too much for Judith's overwrought emotions. She buried her face in her hands and the tears streamed over them without check. Great sobs rent her slight body. The events of two days were culminating in a natural outlet.

Mark crouched beside her, bewildered and distressed. Even Digger sensed her misery and crept to lay across her feet, imparting comfort in the best way he knew. Mark talked to her soothingly, handed her his handkerchief, brushed the golden strands of hair away from her forehead. But still the sobs racked her although she tried hard to stop them. Judith hated to cry. It was the kind of thing which put her at a disadvantage. At last Digger could stand no more and raising his head, he howled mournfully in sympathy. Miraculously, Judith's tears ceased and she lifted her head to give Mark a watery smile. Mark patted Digger's head. 'Good boy!' he said. 'Feel better now?' he asked Judith. 'Don't cry any more—you're only upsetting Digger.'

She blew her nose sharply and pulled herself together. Mark poured hot, fragrant coffee into one of the delicate cups and brought it over to her. 'You'd better drink this,' he said. Obediently she took the cup.

'I'm sorry,' she said unsteadily. 'I'm not usually given to tears—it ruins one's face.'

He bent down to look at her closely.

'Not a single blotch,' he assured her emphatically. 'You're still lovely.' He took out his cigarette case and handed it to her. Gratefully, she inhaled the soothing smoke and felt herself grow calm under its influence.

She looked up at Mark. 'Well, where do we go from here?'

'Where indeed?' he returned. 'I would suggest bed for you, Judith...'

'That isn't what I meant,' she said quickly.

He evaded her eyes. 'I know very well what you meant, my dear. We can't go back, of course—no matter how attractive the past may seem, it's never wise to turn back the pages. We'll have to see what the future brings, I suppose.'

'But you'll never forget the past,' Judith said bitterly.

He kicked a log further on to the fire. His back was towards Judith. 'It isn't the past yet,' he said in a low voice. 'It's still very much with us.'

CHAPTER VII

Judith watched Mark and sadness fought with tenderness in her face. He had Mandy, the five year old, on his lap and Michael crouched on the floor at his feet. Both children were ready for bed, newly-bathed, their small healthy faces glowing in the firelight; Michael's fair hair, close-cropped, stood up damply on his head. Mark was brushing the long silken curls of the little girl. As he did so, he was telling them a story about Digger, the spaniel, whose ears pricked up at every mention of his name. Judith knew that Mark was not a child-lover: he had told her that he had no desire to become a parent; yet he had immeasurable patience with these two children and they openly adored him.

Her father sat in a comfortable armchair

beside the fire, his old pipe clenched between his teeth, an evening paper on his lap. He had lost interest in the news and now studied his son-in-law, occasionally glancing across at Judith. He was puzzled by the slight sadness which tinged her eyes and by the faint droop of her lips. Since they had arrived at the Lodge, she had tried hard to give the impression of happiness, but Clifford was not deceived by the act. He was a shrewd man and very far-seeing where Judith was concerned. He wondered if she was disappointed in her marriage, if Mark Debenham left much to be desired as a husband. Clifford could only know his son-in-law as a man he respected and admired. But as a husband, as a lover—he mentally shrugged. There was some coldness of nature about him, some reserve in his character—and Judith had always been so impulsive, so affectionately eager and warm-hearted. Was it possible that she felt rebuffed by Mark's external coldness? External, for Clifford felt sure that the man possessed great, perhaps unplumbed as yet, depths of feeling and warmth.

At the end of the story, Mary rose from the settee, putting aside the dress she was embroidering for her daughter. She was a pleasant-faced, plump young woman in her late twenties, dark brown hair and brown eyes which smiled easily. Faint touches of grey at her temples were the only sign of the sorrow she had known during her short life. She moved over to Mark and the children and rumpled Michael's hair so that it stood up even more than before.

'Bed for you two,' she announced firmly. 'Thank Uncle Mark for the story.' She smiled at Mark. 'You're very good with them,' she commended. 'I've never known them so obedient—or so quiet as it nears their bedtime.'

Michael scrambled to his feet. Mark, still holding the little girl, rose. 'Shall I take you up, Mandy?'

'Please, please, please!' she answered

eagerly, and Mark laughed. He glanced over at Judith and their eyes met. He looked away quickly and turned towards the door.

'Come on, young man,' he addressed Michael.

They left the room in a flurry of noise and excitement. Judith picked up a magazine and riffled idly through the pages. Clifford bit hard on the stem of his pipe and studied her intently. She was restless and on edge: he was sure she was unhappy. It suddenly stuck him how seldom she exchanged remarks with Mark. Conversation was frequently general but Judith never directly addressed her husband and although he was never impolite, he rarely turned to her with a comment or asked her opinion. She smoked a cigarette with nervous, frequent inhalations.

He leaned forward. 'What's the matter, Judith? Can I help in any way?'

She looked up from the magazine sharply. 'Help? Good heavens, Daddy, there's nothing wrong. Why should you think anything's the matter?'

He shrugged slightly. 'Just an impression.'

She laughed. 'Are you imagining things again?' She met his eyes levelly. 'What could be wrong? I'm perfectly happy...'

'Are you?' he cut in quickly.

'Of course.' She changed the subject. 'Mary's looking very well, Daddy.'

'She is, isn't she?' he agreed eagerly. 'She's lost that peaky look.' He tapped his pipe against an ashtray. 'It's the best thing I ever did, you know, my dear—bringing a little happiness to Mary and the children.'

She smiled at him warmly. 'I'm afraid I was rather beastly about it, Daddy—I suppose I was only being selfish.'

He shook his head. 'Not selfish. You're like your mother, that's all. You just don't like changes. I think you would have been quite content to keep house for me for some years to come, wouldn't you?' Then he smiled. 'Until you wanted to get married, of course—then poor old Daddy would have been left in the lurch!'

'I should have been adult enough to accept Mary sooner and admit that only your happiness mattered,' Judith said stoutly.

'Then you've accepted her now?' Clifford asked with a sly look in his eyes.

'Yes,' Judith admitted. 'I can see that you're happy—and you really do worship her children. I thought you might find them a little too much for you, Daddy.'

He laughed. 'Nonsense! They're giving me back my youth. They needed a father—I'm afraid Mary lacks the authority to control them properly. But they obey me—and I never brandish a rod!'

Judith nodded. 'Michael is a handful at times, I should imagine.' That haunting sadness was back in her eyes when she added: 'Mark seems to have an instinctive way with them both.'

'Mark has the heart of a born father,' Clifford said wisely. He added diffidently:

'Of course, it's early days yet, but I suppose you've discussed having a family.'

Judith's face closed down against him, and he knew that he had touched an old wound. 'As you say, it's early days yet, Daddy.' She rose and crossed to the coffee table. 'Would you care for some fresh coffee? That's surely cold.'

Mark came back into the lounge as she was pouring the hot, fragrant liquid. 'That lad needs taming,' he addressed Clifford. 'You've a long job on your hands, sir.'

Clifford smiled. 'I've tamed worse,' he said quietly. 'Michael simply ran wild after his father died and Mary had to work to keep them all.'

'Of course—I'd forgotten your school-master days,' Mark said with a grin. 'They'll stand you in good stead now.'

'Fresh coffee, Mark?' Judith asked him quietly.

He shook his head. 'No, thanks.' He turned back to Clifford. 'Would you care for a frame or two, sir? I warn you—I'm in good form tonight!'

The two men went off to have their game of snooker and Judith aimlessly drifted back to the fireplace. Taking a cigarette, she bent down to light a taper from the blaze in the hearth.

'You're smoking too much, my sweet!' Casey told her. He had entered the room while her back was turned and she spun round sharply.

He had returned from London the previous day, much chagrined to discover that they had been home from France a few days. Sensitive as always to atmosphere, he knew instinctively that something was wrong between Mark and Judith. It did not matter to him who was at fault—he instantly sided with Judith and felt angry with Mark that he should bring sadness to the lovely eyes and despair to the corners of her sweet mouth.

'Oh, you're back,' she exclaimed obviously.

He grinned. He glanced about the room.

'Where are your guests? It's pathetic to find such a lovely hostess all alone.'

'Well, I'm not alone now,' she retorted. She offered him a cigarette. 'Mark and Daddy are playing snooker.'

Casey made a moué of distaste. 'How very plebeian!' he exclaimed.

'Mary's putting the children to bed.'

He breathed an exaggerated sigh of relief. 'Ah! Reprieve! I wondered if I would escape the horrors of bedtime torments. Last night!' He raised his eyes to the ceiling. 'They really are a passel of brats!'

Judith laughed. 'You know you don't mean that, Casey,' she reproached him. 'Anyway, can two be a passel?'

He shrugged. 'Who knows or cares?' He caught her hand. 'How beautiful you look tonight, Judy—with that air of sweet sadness. Why so sad? Tell your Uncle Casey what the naughty man did to you in Paris that you came home with a broken heart? Did he neglect you for the beauties of the Folies Bergère?'

Judith took her hand away. 'What nonsense you come out with, Casey.' She laughed at him with a light heart for the moment. 'I don't feel at all sad!'

He came closer to her with an air of a conspirator about to divulge a plot. 'This is our first moment alone. Judy, my sweet. Tell me all! Let me be your confidante—your secret will be safe with me. I'll swear to that!' He wet his finger and drew it across his throat dramatically. 'My lips will never reveal it to another!'

She pushed him away. 'What secret?'

'No secret? No sadness? I am undone!' he exclaimed and bowed his head in mock sorrow. 'I was convinced that I had divined misery and despair in your heart.'

'You are a fool!' Judith told him lightly. She took his hand and squeezed his fingers. 'But I love to hear your nonsense, Casey.'

'Fools have always been beloved by queens,' he assured her solemnly. 'And

191

you're my queen, Judy. I lay my heart at your feet as homage.' He lifted her fingers to his lips. Memory surged through her and she snatched her hand away.

'Don't do that, Casey!' she exclaimed. He raised his eyebrows in astonishment. 'Your breath tickles,' she explained quickly, feebly. She moved away from him and sat down on the settee. 'Put some logs on the fire, will you, Casey? It's quite cold in here now.'

Casey crouched down on the hearth and built up the fire with fresh logs. Then he caressed Digger's ears idly, whistling faintly under his breath, looking into the fire. He had sobered suddenly as he was wont to do—all trace of jest vanished completely. After a few minutes, he rose and went over to the piano. Lifting the lid, he ran his fingers idly over the keys, a note here and there.

'Are you going to play?' Judith asked him, her eyes upon his tall, slight figure.

'Perhaps. Come over here, Judy—come

and stand by the piano. I'll play to you,' he assured her.

Amused but faintly puzzled, she did as he asked. He sat down on the piano stool and smiled up at her, his fingers instinctively straying to the keys. The lovely notes of *Liebestraum* rose softly into the air. The haunting melody touched the core of despair in Judith and she dug her nails into her palms. She closed her eyes briefly against the pain. Casey's eyes never left her face. Still playing, he said softly, 'Is it Mark?' She nodded almost imperceptibly. He went on playing. 'I can't bear to know that you're unhappy, Judy,' he told her gently. 'The curve of your cheek, the tilt of your chin, the sweetness of your mouth—they all tell me that you were born for happiness.'

'Happiness is elusive,' she said with bitterness.

'That's why it's so precious.' His fingers were soft on the keys.

'I am unhappy,' she admitted reluctantly.

'But it's my own fault, Casey. No one can help me but myself—and I can't see the way.'

'Does your love blind you?'

'You mean, do I love Mark too much? Do I expect too much?' She looked at him eagerly. This had never occurred to her.

'It isn't possible to love too much—but loving too blindly is wrong,' he told her. 'Don't put Mark on a pedestal, Judy...'

Words tumbled from her. 'No, no, you're wrong, Casey. You're seeing things the wrong way round. It's me—I've toppled from my pedestal.' Her lips twisted bitterly. 'If Mark kept me so high in his estimation! But I've let him down badly, Casey ... that's why I'm unhappy. I've hurt him so much...' She broke off. The music still rose to tear down the barriers of reserve and reveal her naked despair. Their eyes met and there was swift appeal on the one side and swift response on the other. 'Casey, you've known Mark a long time,' she began slowly. 'How can I make him forgive me?'

The music stopped abruptly. Casey rose from the piano and walked over to the fireplace. He said over his shoulder: 'It all depends on the enormity of your misdeeds, my sweet. Mark doesn't forgive easily at the best of times—hurt his pride or hurt him where it really matters—his heart—and he'll make you pay for the rest of your life!'

Judith ran to him. 'Don't say that!' she pleaded. 'I can't bear any more—I can't! He must forgive me—you must help me, Casey.'

He looked into her tense face. 'What have you done?' he asked.

'Hadn't you better ask me?' came Mark's steely voice. Judith swung round. 'It isn't good manners to embarrass a lady, Casey—and I think Judith might be loth to confess her indiscretions.' He came into the room. 'Where did I put my cigarettes?'

Judith picked up the case from the mantelpiece and handed to him numbly. He thanked her with a nod. He turned to Casey. 'I advise you not to ask me, by the way. I'm old-fashioned—I don't discuss my wife with anyone.' With that curt remark, he left them. Casey and Judith exchanged glances.

'Curiouser and curiouser,' quoted Casey. He smiled reassuringly at Judith. 'Don't worry too much, my sweet. Things will work themselves out—they always do.'

'And everything is for the best in the long run?' asked Judith dryly. 'Let's not be trite, Casey. I'm sorry I burdened you with my woes. Will you be "good-mannered" and forget our recent conversation?'

'I would be a cad to embarrass a lady with unwelcome reminiscences,' he replied smoothly. 'All is forgotten.'

'I wish all were forgiven,' she said bitterly. She ran a hand over her eyes.

Mark returned to Clifford with the cigarette case and flicked it open. Clifford shook his head.

'I prefer my old faithful,' he replied, indicating his pipe. 'Shall we set up another frame, Mark?'

Mark blew cigarette smoke into the air. 'Certainly. I'll lay a fiver on the result of this game, sir,' He smiled. 'I never did like losing money—it might improve my play!'

Clifford carefully lined up his cue. 'Was your Paris trip successful?' he asked casually.

'Very. I made a few excellent deals and it was an opportunity to review business in general.'

'You accomplished a lot in a few days,' Clifford remarked and straightened up. Mark eyed the position of the table, considering his play. 'What did Judith do with herself while you were making all this money?'

'She renewed old acquaintances and made a nostalgic tour of Paris.'

'She was very happy there a few years ago.' The elderly eyes twinkled. 'I thought she'd lost her heart to the Congrieve boy—Peregrine Congrieve—but she soon recovered. Did you meet the Congrieves?

197

They're charming people.'

'No,' Mark replied curtly. He stood back from the table so that Clifford could take his shot. 'I think Judith looked them up.'

Clifford chuckled. 'I wonder what she thought of Perry after three years. Probably decided she'd had a lucky escape.'

'Brilliant shot, sir!' applauded Mark. 'I look like losing my fiver!'

They returned to the lounge some time later. Casey had challenged Mary to a card game and was obviously being roundly beaten. He looked up as the two men entered.

'Your wife's a card-sharper, sir,' he addressed Clifford. 'I'm losing pounds!'

Mark laughed. 'That makes two of us, then!' He exchanged glances with Clifford. 'A drink, sir?'

He dispensed drinks all round. Clifford went to stand behind his wife's chair, interested in the card game. Mark stood with his back to the fire, a drink in one hand, a cigarette in the other. He was very thoughtful as he recalled Clifford's remarks about the Congrieves. Was it possible that Judith had sought out Perry Congrieve with the intention of fanning old flames? Had he been the man concerned? He looked down at Judith, trying to reconcile his thoughts with the ideal of her as a woman he had once kept in his heart.

'Did you enjoy your game?' Judith asked him in a brittle voice.

'Very much,' he replied. 'Your father is an excellent player and won both frames.' He absently bent to run his hand over Digger's back and the dog's tail wagged sleepily. Straightening up, his hand accidentally brushed Judith's head and she looked up quickly. Their eyes met for a brief moment, then she dropped her lashes. To Mark's sensitive frame of mind, it seemed a guilty movement and his lips tightened abruptly.

When their game finished, Casey insisted that they should all play cards. Reluctantly, Judith was pressed into the game. Clifford shook his head.

'I prefer to sit by the fire, smoke my pipe, and think my thoughts,' he said genially. 'You young people play, by all means.'

Mark agreed to play and partnered Mary at whist. The game and the evening seemed interminable to Judith. At last it dragged to its weary close. Mary announced that she was tired.

'I'm not surprised,' Casey said lightly. 'Your two children must be very wearying.'

Mary laughed. 'One gets used to them,' she retorted. She rose from the card-table.

Clifford was not long in following her. A last pipe and a drink, desultory conversation with Mark, then he too rose from his comfortable chair and left them.

Casey looked at the older man's departing back and then glanced from Judith to Mark. He moved over to the decanters and poured himself another drink. Mark watched him moodily. Casey carried the glass over to the piano and sat down before

it. Softly, he began to play *Claire de Lune.*
Judith leaned back in her chair and closed
her eyes. Mark stood studying the glowing
end of his cigarette then with a violent
movement he threw it into the fire.

'Isn't it a bit late for that, Casey?' he
demanded.

Casey shrugged and continued to play.
'If music be the food of love...' he quoted.
'Or *music hath charms to sooth the savage
breast...'* He flung an impudent grin
over his shoulder. 'Would either be
appropriate?'

'I hardly think so,' Mark said coldly.

Judith rose abruptly to her feet. 'I'm
going to bed,' she announced.

When the two men were alone, Mark
seemed to relax. He threw himself down
into the armchair that his wife had vacated.
'Come over by the fire, Casey,' he invited.
'I'd like to talk to you.'

Casey played a few more bars, then rose
and closed the lid of the piano. He sat
down in the armchair facing Mark. 'Fire

away,' he said casually.

Mark paused a moment. Then he said: 'What were you and Judith talking about earlier?'

Casey raised a quizzical eyebrow. 'You want me to divulge confidences, old man?'

Mark made an impatient gesture. 'Not if they were confidences. Actually, I can make a fairly accurate guess, if I have to.'

Casey leaned forward. 'I can tell you this—Judith is extremely unhappy and I don't like to see her so depressed without wanting to help.'

'Did she ask for your help?'

'Yes. And my advice. But I can't be much help unless I know what the devil is up between you two.'

'It's the very devil!' exclaimed Mark harshly. The words seemed forced from him as he added: 'While we were in Paris, Judith cleared off with another man. She came back the next day with guilt written all over her and admitted spending the night with him.'

There was a long silence while Casey digested the words. Then he said firmly: 'I don't believe it.'

Mark gave a bitter laugh. 'It is hard to believe of Judith, isn't it?'

'Hard? It's damned impossible!' Casey exclaimed. 'Judith just isn't that sort of woman.'

'Exactly what I would have said.' Mark sank his head in his hands. 'I was worried sick about her,' he said in a low voice. 'I'd no idea where she was—she'd spun me some cock-and-bull story about meeting a girl-friend. When I tried to find her by ringing friends of hers, I found out that her mythical girl-friend wasn't even in Paris and that they hadn't laid eyes on Judith. She claimed to be lunching with them. I didn't sleep all night. I had to go to the gallery in the morning but I was determined that if she hadn't returned by lunch-time, I would go to the Sûreté. My God, Casey—can you imagine the state I was in—the thoughts that passed through my mind? She rang me up during the morning from some village near Versailles and told me she'd be back at the hotel by lunch-time. I raced back there—and saw her driving up to the hotel with this damn Frenchman.' He stopped speaking. Casey rose, went to the decanters and poured a stiff whisky which he handed to Mark without a word. Mark drained it and went on: 'When I taxed her with it, she didn't deny it. She calmly told me that she had spent the night with this man and asked what I was going to do about it?'

Casey bit his lower lip. 'It just doesn't sound like Judith,' he said at last. 'Why should she do such a thing—she's newly-married, she's happy, isn't she?' He ran his fingers through his dark hair. 'I would say she's very happy, Mark—or was until now.' He began to pace up and down. Suddenly a thought struck him. 'She's proud, Mark,' he said eagerly. 'If you accused her, she might not deny it. Some people react to accusation that way. Perhaps she couldn't believe that you would think of her so badly.'

Mark raised his head. The look he flashed his one-time ward was cynical. 'An innocent person goes all out to prove his lack of guilt,' he said firmly. 'Judith acted guiltily, Casey. Believe me, I wanted to believe in her innocence.' He sighed.

'But Judith!' Casey was still incredulous. 'She's the last person one would associate with lies or guilt of that kind.'

Mark slapped his fist into the palm of the other hand. 'What made her do it?' he exclaimed. 'I shall never understand her motives! Have I neglected her so much? Have I been cruel to her? Am I lacking in the necessary attributes of a husband?'

Casey met his eyes squarely. 'You're the only one who can answer those questions, Mark, old man. And as far as I can see, this is the sort of situation where I can't help in any way. It's a matter between you and Judith.' He said diffidently: 'Are you considering divorce?'

'No.' The reply came with swift violence. 'I'll never divorce her. No matter what she does, she's my wife—and she stays married to me.' He looked up at Casey and his inner emotions were naked. 'I need her, Casey,' he said harshly.

Casey kicked a dying log into place. A shower of sparks soared up the chimney. 'Then it might be a good thing to forget the Paris episode,' he said slowly. 'You can't live together as strangers—it isn't fair on either of you.'

'Forget it?' Mark demanded. 'Forget the worst night of my life? I'll never forget it.'

'Then at least forgive, if you can't forget,' Casey told him sharply. 'And turn yourself inside out to find where you went wrong. A woman doesn't want another man if her husband makes her happy—unless she's a nymphomaniac and nothing on earth will make me believe that of Judith!'

Mark said nothing. He sat forward in his chair and his eyes were riveted on the glowing embers of the fire. Alexander came into the room. 'I'm sorry, sir,' he said quickly. 'I thought you'd all retired. I came to tidy the room.'

Mark stood up. 'All right, Alexander. We're going up now.' He put a hand on Casey's shoulder. 'Thanks,' he said briefly.

He paused by Judith's door and knocked gently. He waited a moment but there was no reply. With a sigh, he moved on to his own room and went in, closing the door behind him with an air of finality.

CHAPTER VIII

Weeks passed and there was no change in the coolness between Mark and Judith. He was seldom at the Lodge. On the plea of business, he spent most of his time in London, staying at the town flat; when he returned to Hurleigh, he shut himself up for hours, alone in his study but for the faithful Digger.

Time passed slowly for Judith and she suffered a great deal from boredom. Caroline Mallow had gone to Italy to visit friends and Judith saw very little of Allan. Casey had many friends and perhaps it was just as well that Judith did not spend too much time with him. She could not forget Mark's suspicions and there were times when she wondered if he had confided in Casey about the Paris episode. The young man was always attentive and charming to her, and he rattled off as much nonsense as ever, but sometimes she caught his eyes upon her and their expression was puzzled and watchful.

He was torn between his devotion to Mark and the affection he bore Judith. He watched her carefully, noting her continued unhappiness, worried by her lack of life, seeking some sign of guilt in her demeanour yet at the same time hoping for proof of her innocence in her words or actions. He did not mention their conversation again to Mark and he respected the fact that the story had been told him in strict confidence.

Casey felt sure that Mark was wrong in his attitude. Perhaps he was justified in his anger and his disappointment, yet Casey could not visualize Judith in the rôle of unfaithful wife. There were times when he knew an impulsive urge to chide Mark for letting things drift on in such a manner. He longed to remind him that life was too short for grudges: that there was enough unhappiness and misunderstanding in the world without allowing it to spoil personal lives; that a man and his wife could not continue to live as strangers and expect their marriage to last any length of time.

Casey was still in love with Judith but he kept his secret from her if not from Mark. He would never betray Mark's trust in any way and it was for this reason that he spent more and more time with the Ancells and his other friends. It was difficult to be with Judith, knowing her pain and unhappiness, and not long to comfort her and in so doing accidentally reveal the depths of his own feelings. No, he told himself firmly, Judith must never suspect that he loved her and he schooled himself carefully to the realization that his love was of no avail. In time perhaps, he would find consolation in another woman's arms but his love was too deep and disturbing at the moment for him to be able to look at another woman without unconsciously comparing her with

Judith to her disadvantage. So he kept his emotions in check and the only sign of his affection was in his sympathetic kindness and the light-hearted companionship he offered her.

Judith began to lose weight: she slept badly and had little appetite. To a casual observer, she was as lovely as always. But to Casey's watchful and sensitive eyes, signs of strain appeared in her face. The skin seemed too finely-drawn over the delicately-etched bones of her fair face; she skilfully applied cosmetics yet still he detected the faint traces of violet shadows beneath the blue eyes. Her lips drooped slightly and the tilt of her chin had lost its unconscious arrogance.

Judith could not believe that this present state of affairs could continue. It was incredible that she and her husband were almost strangers. Mark was always coldly courteous and attentive but there was no warmth in his eyes when he looked at her or in his voice when he spoke. She sometimes wondered why she stayed on at the Lodge. Bitterly she reminded herself that divorce was not the only way to end a marriage. No law forced her to live in her husband's house. But always the hope that one day the difficulties would be smoothed out prevented her from packing her cases and leaving Mark. Though she was sick at heart and in mind because of his coldness and his stubborn refusal to consider any explanation but the one he had instinctively assumed, Judith knew she still loved Mark dearly and it was this love which gave her the courage to carry on, to defy the apparent failure of their marriage and to show a brave front to the world.

Mark was no happier than his wife. He threw himself into an orgy of hard work, trying to forget the hurt and the anger, waiting for the day when he could readily forgive Judith and return to the Lodge with a light heart and open arms.

One morning, a discreet tap on the door

made Judith look up from her letters. Alexander came in and his usual calm demeanour seemed disturbed.

'Madam,' he said agitatedly. 'Will you come—it's Mr Casey!'

Judith pushed away her writing things. 'What is it, Alexander?' She had taken little notice of the noise outside the house, the sound of cars driving up and the conversation that ensued when Alexander hurried to answer the peremptory summons of the bell. But the manservant's agitation communicated itself to her and she rose to her feet.

'They've brought Mr Casey home by car, madam—it seems he fell from his horse while hunting.'

Judith wrinkled her forehead. She knew that Casey had gone out with the Ancells on a hunt. It was one of his favourite pastimes.

She hurried into the hall. David Ancell turned, his pleasant face anxious and disturbed.

'Judith!' he exclaimed. 'Is Mark at home?'

She shook her head. 'I'm afraid not. He's been in Town for the last few days. Where is Casey?'

'Two of the chaps are bringing him in. He's badly hurt, I'm afraid. I don't know much about these things—I left a message for Morley but he's out on a case. I think it's his back, Judith.'

She caught her breath. 'How did it happen?'

'He was thrown—that ridiculous hedge at Long End. He insisted on Jason taking it at the highest point—the damn horse stopped short and Casey went straight over his head. I was close behind and got to him straight away.'

'I must phone Mark,' Judith said decisively. 'He'll get hold of the right man. Casey will have to be examined thoroughly—Morley won't know enough about the spine to be much use.'

At that moment, they brought Casey

in, carrying him carefully on a makeshift stretcher. He smiled at Judith a little crookedly. She went over to him and took his hand.

'Now what have you been doing?' she asked him lightly but she was torn with anxiety.

'My own fault entirely,' he assured her. 'Jason had more sense than I did—he knew he'd never make that jump.'

'Are you in much pain?'

He shook his head very slightly. 'No, that's the funny thing. I can't move my legs at all—it must be my back, blast it!—but nothing hurts.'

Judith and David exchanged glances. Both recognized this to be a bad sign where the back was concerned. Alexander threw open the doors of the lounge and indicated that Casey should be carried into the warm room. Carefully, they transferred him from the stretcher to the settee. Judith hurriedly brought brandy over to him and insisted that he drink it. He was very pale and his eyes searched hers as if in reassurance for Casey was no fool and he knew well enough that the damage might be more extensive than seemed.

'When you telephone Mark, ask him to contact Keiller, will you? He's the man to examine me. Perhaps Mark can persuade him to come immediately. I don't want old Morley poking and prodding me.' He forced a grin. 'Morley treats all his patients as though they were one of those damn pigs he breeds!'

It was some little time before Judith could persuade David Ancell and the others who had insisted on coming to the Lodge with him and Casey that they could do no more for the injured man. Reluctantly, they left as Morley's car turned into the drive.

Casey caught Judith's hand. 'Don't let the old fool in,' he said quickly. 'Tell him I'm perfectly all right—just a few bruises...'

But Alexander had already admitted the 'old fool' and Dr Morley, an elderly,

216

capable man with kindly eyes, silvery hair and a devotion to his pigs, stood in the doorway.

'I hear you've had a toss, young man,' he said easily.

'It isn't the first,' Casey assured him lightly.

'I know that very well,' Morley replied dryly. 'But from all accounts, it's more serious than usual.' He smiled at Judith. 'Good morning, Mrs Debenham! I hope you aren't too worried about Casey—he's had many a hard knock and he usually survives to tell the tale.'

Judith smiled weakly. 'I'll leave you to run your experienced eyes over him, Dr Morley. I'll phone Mark,' she told Casey quickly and headed for the door.

'I can hear his immediate reaction now,' grinned Casey. 'He'll call me a blasted young fool!'

Judith closed the door quietly behind her and stood for a moment or two, resting against the polished panels. She would have to find the right words to tell Mark of the accident, to impress upon him that it was necessary to call in the specialist Casey had mentioned, yet to reassure him that Casey seemed in little or no pain and it was possibly not a serious injury.

She glanced at the slim gold watch on her wrist. Would Mark be still at the flat or at the gallery? It was possible that he couldn't be found at either, for he moved around London a lot on business, visiting other galleries, carrying out private deals.

She dialled the number of the flat. She waited for what seemed an eternity before at last the receiver was lifted. A familiar voice gave the number and Judith stiffened, tense with shock and suspicion.

'Caroline! Is that you?' she demanded.

'Judith!' She turned away from the telephone; 'Mark darling, it's Judith.' Then, again to the girl who leaned against the table in the hall for sudden support, jealousy tearing her heart to pieces: 'How are you, my dear? Long time no see! I'm back in England at last—tell my disreputable brother that I'll see him at the week-end, will you?'

'When did you get back from Italy?' Judith asked, forcing a casual note to her voice.

'A few days ago.' Caroline laughed. 'I should have let you know I was back, but I've been so busy. It's rather lovely in London at the moment. But crowded! It's impossible to get a decent suite in any hotel. Mark was an angel and suggested I use the flat as my base—I came over with some charming Italians and they're using me as guide...' Her voice trailed off. 'Oh, here's Mark now.'

Judith waited, an icy hand clutched at her heart. Caroline was staying at the flat—and Mark had suggested it. She had answered the phone with apparent ease of custom and there had been an air of possessiveness about her words to Mark which Judith had overheard.

'Hallo, Judith.' He was deliberately cool,

very conscious of Caroline at his side who stood, a cigarette between slender fingers, watching him with provocative eyes and an inscrutable smile touching her lips.

'Mark, can you come home?' The words were forced from stiff lips. In ordinary circumstances, she would never make such a plea—particularly with the knowledge that Caroline was at the flat and all the suspicions that knowledge aroused. But Casey had to be considered and Mark would never forgive her if she kept such information from him.

Mark frowned. 'Is anything wrong?' he asked quickly. 'I'm very busy at the moment—I have a big deal on and I'm only waiting to see one particular man...'

'It's Casey,' she interrupted roughly. She explained briefly and added: 'Do you know this man Keiller?'

Mark replied swiftly: 'Yes. He's a spinal specialist—I'll get hold of him right away. I hope to God he's free and will agree to come back with me. Don't worry,

Judith—you say that Morley is there. He's a sound man, he'll give good advice. I'll get back as soon as I can.' He hung up briefly and then dialled the number of Keiller's home.

Judith looked at the receiver in her hand and then slowly cradled it. For the moment, her anxiety over Casey had faded. She was more concerned with the presence of Caroline in the London flat and with the uncontrollable jealousy which surged through her whole being.

When Mark arrived, a few hours later, not only was he accompanied by the specialist, but Caroline too followed them into the house. She hurried over to Judith.

'What a worry for you, my dear! How is he?'

Their eyes met and Judith felt a slight flush rise in her cheeks as the woman's sophistication impressed itself once more on her. Caroline had the unhappy knack of making Judith feel a mere child and inconsequential. She was looking regal and lovely, the freshness of the day having whipped a faint colour into her sunburned cheeks, her auburn curls slightly dishevelled. Her suit was impeccably tailored in hyacinth blue tweed.

Judith made no reply. She brushed past Caroline and walked over to Mark. He looked down at her absently and then introduced her to Sir Martin Keiller. The great man acknowledged the introduction but was obviously impatient to get on with his examination of Casey. Mark took him into the lounge where Casey still lay; Morley had given him a sedative which the young man had refused to take, insistent that he was not in pain and needed no drugs. Caroline walked over to the fire that blazed in the hearth and slowly drew off her gloves.

'Martin's very busy,' she said idly, 'but he readily agreed to come with us when I explained the situation. He's a great friend of mine, you know.'

Judith glanced at her cursorily. 'I'm sure Mark could have persuaded him if it had been necessary.'

'I had to come,' Caroline went on. 'Poor Casey—he's such a reckless young devil! I've always warned him that one day he'll break his neck on Jason.'

Judith ran a hand over her golden head. She felt untidy and coltish against the smooth sophistication of Caroline Mallow. Her black woollen dress seemed suddenly schoolgirlish and shabby. She moved to the bellpush that was discreetly cut into the carvings of the panelled fireplace.

'Do sit down, Caroline,' she invited politely. 'I'll order coffee.'

Caroline drew up a comfortable chair, sat down and elegantly crossed her slim legs. She was so very poised and confident. Judith had never been so conscious of the woman's striking attractions. Perhaps the atmosphere and climate of Italy had brought out new beauty in her—and Judith could not help wondering if Mark had suddenly grown susceptible to Caroline's beauty.

'How are you?' Judith asked slowly. It was difficult to make small talk while her confused thoughts dwelt not only on Casey and the examination which was taking place but also on her husband and the mystery of Caroline's presence at the flat. 'You're looking very well,' she ungraciously added.

'I'm blooming with health,' Caroline replied easily. She took a slim cigarette case from her handbag but before she could open it, Judith presented the small silver box which she took from the mantelpiece. Both women lighted cigarettes.

'And how was Italy?'

Caroline shivered delicately. 'Warmer than England,' she said emphatically. She slanted her grey-green eyes towards Judith's face and their expression was carefully veiled. 'Mark seems to spend a lot of time in Town these days,' she said casually. 'From something he said, it would seem that he's never at home.'

'He's very busy,' Judith replied shortly as Alexander entered carrying the silver tray with the coffee pot and the delicate china coffee-cups already arranged upon it. Judith sat down and poured the coffee.

Caroline waited until the man had withdrawn. Then she said idly: 'Still, you've always got Casey on the spot. I'm sure he takes good care of you.'

Judith felt swift anger at the innuendo behind Caroline's words. But the hostility which still sprang to life whenever they met was as yet undeclared and Judith would not give her the satisfaction of knowing that her remark had found a target.

'I wish he would take good care of himself,' she replied heavily, ignoring the innuendo. 'Heaven knows what he's done now.'

'Casey is like a cat—he has nine lives and he hasn't exhausted them all yet,' Caroline assured her easily. 'Martin knows what he's doing—Casey will be all right, if it's humanly possible for Martin to do anything.' She sat back, stirring her coffee idly, and her eyes were on the anxious, pale face of the woman who was Mark Debenham's wife. Judith nervously smoked her cigarette. A silence fell between them. Caroline noted the signs of strain in the youthful face and her eyes narrowed. Surely that slim figure had grown a little thinner since she was last at the Lodge? And there was a lack of light in the deep-blue eyes which disturbed Caroline who had a fund of warm human sympathy behind the cool, sophisticated veneer. Mark's continued absence from Hurleigh had not escaped Caroline's notice. Knowing Mark so well, she could sense his unhappiness and the dissatisfaction he felt with his marriage. Her keen eyes missed nothing. It worried her that Mark, of whom she had always been so fond, should be unhappy and strained, obviously working too hard in an effort to forget some inner anxiety.

Caroline leaned forward in her seat and

was about to fire a question at Judith in her usual impulsive manner, moved by a sudden stir of sympathy, when the lounge doors opened and Mark came out with the specialist.

Judith poured coffee for the two men and they stood talking about Casey for some minutes. It appeared that Sir Martin was anxious about the spinal nerves which had possibly been damaged. He advised Casey's immediate removal to London where an operation might be performed if necessary.

Some time later, an ambulance arrived at the Lodge to take Casey and Sir Martin back to London. The younger man was inclined to think the whole thing an unnecessary amount of fuss over a mild fall. If he were anxious about his lack of easy movement, he did not show it and he assured Mark until the very moment of departure that an indefinite sojourn in a London nursing-home was a waste of money and that his injuries, if any, were scarcely worth Sir Martin's skill and experience.

Judith bent over and kissed Casey's cheek very tenderly. 'I wish you'd be good and submit that you know nothing at all about it,' she told him lightly. 'Sir Martin wouldn't bother with you if there were nothing wrong, Casey.'

He grinned. 'What a waste of the hunting season!' he exclaimed. 'Lying in bed flat on my back... You'll come and visit me, won't you, my sweet? Or I shall die of boredom.'

She promised that she would visit him frequently and supply him with everything he wanted while he was in the nursing-home. At last, the ambulance drove away from the Lodge. Mark turned to Judith.

'I might as well stay the night now I'm here,' he said casually. 'But I must go up to London first thing in the morning.' He addressed Caroline. 'What about you, Caro? Weren't you meeting your Italian friends this evening?'

She nodded. 'I'll drive up later,' she said. 'It will be useful to have the car in Town anyway.' She smoothed her gloves. 'I'll walk home,' she announced. 'I can use the exercise.' She set off down the drive, with a gay wave of her hand.

Mark and Judith went back into the house and entered the lounge. He went over to the decanters and poured a drink. 'Do you want one?' he asked casually.

'No, thank you. It's a little early, isn't it?'

He shrugged. 'I need this,' he announced and tossed the contents of the glass down his throat with a quick movement. Then he refilled the glass. 'Bit of a shock about Casey,' he said quietly. 'Blasted young fool—he's always smashing himself up. If it isn't the car, it's a horse.' He glanced across at her. Judith stood by the fire, her head bowed, her hands by her side. She seemed very dispirited. Mark said sharply: 'Don't worry too much about him, Judith—he's strong

229

and young. In Keiller's hands, he'll soon recover.'

She nodded. Dully she said: 'There's an invitation to the Ancells for next week, Mark. Joy Ancell is getting engaged.'

'Yes, I know. I ran into Keith in Town. Do you want to go to the party?'

She glanced at him. 'Will you be home?'

'I'm not sure...' he began.

'Perhaps you'll prefer to stay at the flat—with Caroline,' she said abruptly.

He frowned. 'What do you mean by that remark?'

She raised her head and her eyes were cold. 'I imagine my meaning must be obvious.'

He moved to stand near her by the fire. His eyes narrowed. 'I don't care for the implication, Judith.'

'I don't particularly care to telephone the flat and find Caroline so much at home there,' she rejoined. 'She told me she was staying there.'

'That's right,' he said coolly. 'I suggested

she should use the flat for a few days. London is full of tourists.'

'You must find her company very entertaining,' she sneered.

'I don't see very much of her.' He was determined not to be drawn into an argument.

'Then she has my fullest sympathy. I happen to be in the same boat.'

He looked at her sharply. 'Are you lonely? Is life too dull here for you, Judith?'

She shrugged. 'I'm all right. I should hate you to be worried about me, Mark.' Her tone belied her words.

'My business will be finished by next week. I'll come home for a while, then,' he told her. He looked into her face. 'You're looking pale,' he said abruptly. 'Why don't you go to Pelham for a few days? The change would be good for you and your father will be pleased to see you.'

Judith flashed at him: 'I shall go away when you come home? Is that what you mean? Is it so unbearable to live with me, Mark?'

'There's certainly little joy attached to your company,' he retorted brutally.

'Is that entirely my fault?' she asked him in a low voice.

He felt a touch of shame. 'No,' he admitted. 'I'm afraid I'm very difficult to live with just now, Judith.' He began to pace up and down, his lips taut and grim. 'We can't go on like this,' he said abruptly. 'Would you like me to arrange a separation, Judith?'

'Is that what you want?' she asked dully.

He shrugged. 'I've been thinking it might be the best thing, my dear. After all, to all intents and purposes, we're practically separated now. Business takes me away from you and when we're together, there's little happiness for either of us.'

'Because you won't forgive me,' she cried. 'I can't understand you, Mark. How long can a man go on being bitter and angry? I can't bear this hell any more.'

'That's why a separation certainly seems the only way out,' he said calmly. 'I hoped time would make a difference to my feelings, but I can't forgive you, Judith. It's impossible.'

'Aren't you human?' she demanded bitterly. 'Have you never made mistakes? I only lied to you—have you never lied to anyone? I swear I did nothing else—you've never given me the chance to tell what happened that night...'

'I won't give you the chance to spin me another pack of lies,' he said grimly. 'I'm not interested in hearing your version of what happened, Judith.'

'You prefer to believe that I could spend the night with another man when I'd only been married to you a month?'

'Isn't that what happened?' he asked her coolly.

'No!' she exclaimed desperately. 'I was ill...'

He turned on his heel and walked out of

233

the room. Judith stared after him, helpless, miserable—then she buried her head in her hands and began to cry.

Mark stood in the hall with his hands still on the wooden knob of the door. He was torn between the desire to go back to her, to take her in his arms and assure her that he would believe whatever she told him as long as they could find some measure of happiness together, and the anger which still possessed him whenever he thought of that night in Paris and the man she had been with. He heard the bitter sobs which tore the silence of the room behind him and he knew that they could not go on like this. He went into the lounge.

'Stop crying, Judith,' he said firmly. 'You'll make yourself ill. Here, take this...' He handed her his handkerchief and she dabbed helplessly at her eyes and cheeks. He lifted her chin with a stern hand and frowned to see the dark shadows, the tautness of her cheeks and the hollow misery in her eyes. 'Crying doesn't do any good,' he told her firmly. 'Pull yourself together, my dear. You're much too sensitive...'

'Sensitive!' she cried. 'Am I supposed to smile when you're deliberately cruel to me? Do you think it doesn't hurt me when you go away for days at a time and avoid my company when you are here? You're breaking my heart, Mark!'

'You've only yourself to blame for that,' he told her harshly.

'How can you be so hard—so cruel?' She began to cry again. Tears came so easily to her now and she could not control them.

'Weren't you cruel to me?' he asked quietly.

'But you didn't care—you've never cared!' she sobbed bitterly. 'And I've always loved you so much—don't kill my love! Forgive me—let me be happy again. I don't care if you don't love me—but for God's sake, Mark, don't hate me!'

She caught his hand and carried it to her lips.

'I don't hate you,' he said oddly. 'Do you think I would be so angry if I didn't care, my dear? Would I have worried about you so much? Would it matter to me how many men you want if I didn't care for you, Judith?' He took her hands. She barely came to his shoulder and gently, he brushed back a few golden strands from her face—and then, with a groan, he pulled her into his arms and held her close, burying his lips against her hair. She clung to him, her slight body trembling, thrilling to his touch. He thought with pity how frail she seemed and his heart went out to her. Poor Judith! Whatever she had done, surely he had punished her enough—he was punishing himself, too, by staying away from her, by pushing away all desire for her, all need of her loveliness... His lips strayed to her temple, to her cheek, and she turned her head so that their lips met. Her mouth was tremulous

236

and sweet and a flame of passion leaped in him. He held her closer still and his kisses grew more demanding—then a vision came flashing to his memory and he saw her get out of the car outside the Hôtel le Grand and he saw again the attractive young man who leaned forward to close the taxi door and watch her walk into the hotel. With an instinctive movement, he released her.

She raised lovely eyes to his face and what she read in his expression hurt her intolerably. He turned away and stared into the leaping flames of the fire.

'I'm sorry, Judith,' he said in a low voice. 'It's useless—I can't forget...' His voice trailed off.

Her hands were clenched by her sides. 'Very well, Mark.' Her voice was lifeless. 'You'd better arrange the separation you seem to want.'

It was her turn to walk across the large and attractive room in silence. The door closed behind her slim figure and Mark threw himself into a chair, his mouth taut and his body tense. Sensing the despondency in his master, Digger padded over to him and laid his chin on Mark's knee, his whole body quivering with sympathy...

CHAPTER IX

Mark returned to London that same night. He drove his car recklessly, feverishly, his thoughts with Judith and the hopeless situation which existed between them. Despite her last words to him, he hesitated to contact his lawyer. Separation was so final: not as final as divorce, it was true, but it was still an admission that two people had failed to live together amicably. His pride revolted against the decision. Pride and his need of Judith.

He had woken to the realization that his wife was the most important part of his life. He loved her with all his being yet he had thought he would never know what love could mean. Bitterly now he remembered his assertion that he was immune to such emotion. Love had come late to him but its force and effect were devastating. With the love had come a jealousy that threatened to destroy him and the happiness he could have known with Judith. It was an uncontrollable savage jealousy which prevented him from forgiving or forgetting her disloyalty and filled him with the insane desire to hurt her as she had hurt him.

But in some sane moments, he wondered what was the point of being jealous now that the episode was past. He no longer doubted Judith's loyalty. He believed the lesson had been harsh enough to prevent her from making the same mistake again. He was sure that she still loved him—yet he could not look forward to a future with her in which the ghost of Peregrine Congrieve did not raise his spectral head.

He went to see Casey. Sir Martin was still waiting for the results of the interminable x-rays which had been so necessary but his opinion of Casey's condition was not an encouraging one and Mark went into

Casey's private room with a heavy heart. It pained him to see the young man, usually so active and gay, flat on his back and helpless.

He was cheerful but bored and convinced that he was perfectly well. The complete absence of pain was the one thing which troubled Sir Martin but which reassured Casey that the fall had done very little damage. He was impatient to be up and about again and irritable because he found it impossible to move his limbs as his will directed. It was his theory, which he explained to Mark, that the shock of the fall had temporarily dulled the nerves of the spine and that the enforced rest he now had to undergo would cure that in the shortest possible time. In the face of his incurable optimism, it was difficult to stress Sir Martin's anxiety or to point out that it might be months before Casey was off his back, if ever. Mark could not bear to think that Casey might be doomed to spend many years as an invalid.

Casey demanded to know when Judith was going to visit him. 'Why didn't she travel up with you?' he asked, more than a little puzzled.

'She'll probably be in Town soon,' Mark assured him. There was a tautness about him, some note in his voice that informed Casey that all was not well. He lay back on his pillows and raised one eyebrow in query.

'Are things still as strained between you?' he demanded. 'Haven't you patched up your differences yet?' There was a note of exasperation in his voice.

Mark shrugged. 'I doubt if we will,' he said wearily. There was no point in keeping anything back from Casey. He was a persistent young man and he would know eventually. 'We've decided to separate,' he added quietly.

There was a long silence. Casey's eyes had darkened and he kept his gaze intently on Mark's serious face. His thoughts were rapid but his expression inscrutable. His love for Judith had not changed in any way. It was natural that his heart should leap at the news with hope that one day he and Judith ... but here he paused. Judith loved Mark. It was evident in her demeanour, in her voice when she spoke of her husband, in her unhappiness at the situation between them. There would never be any chance for him, Casey reminded himself. He was suddenly angry with Mark because this would mean fresh sorrow for Judith.

'So you've let matters drift that far,' he said at last and there was more than a hint of contempt in his voice. 'Does Judith agree that separation is the only solution to your problems?'

Mark shrugged. 'I imagine so.' His voice was dull. 'There really isn't much point in our marriage as it is at the moment, Casey. One can only assume that it was a mistake from the very start. Obviously Judith wasn't happy or contented or the Paris incident would never have occurred.'

Casey sighed deeply and with exasperation. 'I often wonder if you ever had the whole truth on that business, old man. Maybe I'm prejudiced where Judith is concerned...'

Mark interrupted. 'Of course you are! I've known for ages how you feel about her, Casey.'

Casey was suddenly grim. 'Then you'll understand that I'm only concerned with her happiness. Illicit love affairs just aren't in Judith's line—are you so blind with jealousy that you can't see that?'

Mark rose abruptly and thrust his hands deep into his trouser pockets. 'Look here, Casey—we've had all this out before. It's rather ancient history and it doesn't really have any bearing on the situation now.'

'Of course it does!' Casey was emphatic. 'How can it be ancient history when it's affecting your marriage at this very moment?' He paused. 'Give me a cigarette, will you, Mark?' He gave a lop-sided grin. 'Mine are out of reach, I'm afraid.'

Without comment, Mark produced his case and put a cigarette between Casey's lips. Then he flicked his lighter into life. Casey inhaled with obvious satisfaction and then nodded. Mark removed the cigarette and held it between long, strong fingers. Casey thanked him with a brief smile. Then he went on: 'If you're going to allow one brief episode to ruin both your lives, then I call that pure folly!' He sighed. 'The trouble is that you and Judith both suffer from an excess of pride. She loves you, Mark—but I shouldn't have to tell you that...' He smiled again with sincere warmth.

Mark studied the glowing end of the cigarette he held. 'I believe that she does,' he said in a low voice. 'God knows I love her desperately.' He gave a sudden laugh, dry and bitter. 'I can't live without her—but I just can't go on living with her!' His lips twisted. 'When I want her most, I can visualize her with Congrieve.' He was convinced that he had been the man concerned. An old love—Paris—a chance meeting or an arranged tête-à-tête—what could be more natural? Except that it was the last thing one would expect of Judith to carry it further than that!

'Stubborn pride!' Casey assured him and indicated that Mark should replace the cigarette between his lips. Exhaling blue-grey smoke, he added: 'The best thing you can do is forget the past and make a fresh start, Mark, old man. That's my advice for what it's worth. Otherwise, you'll never know any happiness—and you'll break Judith's heart.' A pause then he said coldly: 'I'll never forgive you for the last, Mark. Judith is too fine a person to suffer in the way that you're making her suffer. Perhaps she did go off the rails with that chap—but it could easily have been you and Caroline and we all know that she's given you many opportunities. Would you have broken up your marriage for her?'

'No!' Mark's answer was firm.

'Then why let a stranger do it for you?'

Mark was just leaving when Casey said: 'By the way, I understand Caroline's at your flat. She telephoned this morning and said she'll come to see me tomorrow.'

There was nothing in his tone or his words but Mark suddenly flared into anger. 'Yes, Caroline's at my flat—and I'm sleeping at the Club! If that's one of the opportunities you referred to, I assure you I'm not taking advantage of it!'

'No offence, old man,' Casey assured him. 'It just occurred to me to wonder if Judith knew that Caroline's staying there.'

'Yes, she does.' His voice was taut.

'Well, I'm sure she understands that you're spending your nights at the Club and not with Caroline—or didn't you make that clear to her?'

Mark stood by the bed. He stared down at Casey. 'Just what are you getting at, Casey?'

'I'm simply puzzled that Judith should agree to a separation when I know darn well it's the last thing she wants. She's always hoped that one day everything would come right between you. But if she thought—if you gave her the impression that you and Caroline—oh, well, it's just a thought that flitted through my mind,' he said casually.

Mark frowned. 'Judith wouldn't suspect me,' he said slowly. 'She's always trusted me—and I've never given her cause to doubt my loyalty.'

Casey nodded. 'I dare say it was a great shock to her when she found out that you suspected her of the same thing,' he said lightly. 'After all, she could offer you the same arguments, Mark.'

Mark left him some minutes later. He drove back to the gallery where he found an old friend and client waiting for him. During the discussion and sale, and the lunch that followed, he found it difficult to concentrate on present matters. His thoughts were still with Casey and their conversation.

It was easy for outsiders, no matter

how close they were or how concerned for one's welfare, to give advice or opinions of personal problems. But it was not so easy for the individual to carry out such advice. Mark had tried to forget the past. He desperately wanted to make a fresh start but his pride and his memory stirred up bitter jealousy. He knew that Casey was right on at least one point. Without Judith, he would never have any happiness.

He returned to his office. He sat at his desk, not attempting to concentrate on the papers which his secretary had put before him. Almost against his will, his hand strayed to the telephone and he picked up the receiver. He was suddenly filled with the longing to hear Judith's voice. His fingers dialled the number unsteadily and his heart thudded as painfully as a boy's. His love for Judith suddenly seemed to be the only important thing in the world and it was an agony of waiting before he was connected to the Lodge.

He listened to the ringing tone, impatiently tapping his fingers on the desk or toying with his fountain pen. If only he could suppress his violent jealousy and forget his bitter pride. Supposing he were to appeal to Judith to agree to a new beginning...

At last he heard Alexander's voice giving the number. 'Oh, Alexander! Is Mrs Debenham there?'

A few minutes later Judith came to the telephone. 'Mark?' Her voice was hard. 'You just caught me in time—I'm catching the twelve-thirty train.'

He was suddenly tense. 'Where are you going?'

'To Pelham for a few days,' she told him casually though her heart beat painfully. 'I'll let you know after that.'

'But why?' he demanded. 'What's the idea, Judith?'

'I think it's the only thing to do, Mark,' she replied coolly and he could not know from her tone that there were unshed tears sparkling behind the golden lashes. 'I've no wish to stay here any longer—and surely it will ease the situation for you.'

'You seem to have made up your mind,' he said curtly.

'Yes. I have. I'll write to you in a few days, Mark. Tell Casey that I'm sorry I can't visit him yet but as soon as I return to London I'll see him.' For a few minutes, in stilted tones, they discussed Casey, then Judith rang off with a hurried explanation that she might miss her train. Mark sat very still then he replaced the receiver slowly and his heart was very heavy. No chance now of a new beginning. Judith was ready to admit that their marriage had been a mistake and she had wasted no time in pulling up stakes. But he could not believe it was all for the best. Her decision had stunned him, driving all coherent thought from him, and he had been unable to say the words which would prevent her from taking such a step...

Judith had spent the night in a dull

wakefulness. She felt a stunned resignation that her marriage was a complete failure. She tried to stir up resentment against Mark but she was devoid of all emotion. Even the love she had borne him seemed to have lost its potency, its depth—and she felt that he had killed emotion in her by his cruel indifference to her breaking heart. Yet she could understand his point of view. With barren spirit, she reviewed their marriage.

It had been absolute folly to meet Perry again by common consent, to encourage him and his attentions, to lie to Mark about the whole affair which had been so innocent. She should have insisted that he hear the true explanation of those hours away from Paris. It seemed incredible that for nearly three months such a state of affairs had existed between them and she realized that they had both been foolish. Mark was a man of deep integrity and he had an instinctive aversion to deceit. It was natural that he had been angry and bitter about her disloyalty. But there was no excuse for the stupid, stubborn pride which had kept her from clearing herself of the charge which he had laid at her door. It was a childish reaction to the hurt he caused her and it had been wicked to let him believe his accusation a true one.

Was it true that Mark had turned to Caroline because he was disappointed in his wife? Judith could not help thinking along these lines.

She remembered the many times that Caroline had hinted at her long friendship with Mark, a friendship that had almost blossomed into love until Judith had come into his life and taken him from her. Oh, Caroline had never said as much but her meaning had been obvious, Judith told herself with bitter lines about her mouth. The rift in their marriage must have been a heaven-sent opportunity to Caroline. Had she heard of it through friends and hastened back to England to console Mark? All this and many other things seethed through Judith's brain that night.

Her presence at the flat needed a better explanation than Mark had cared to give her—and jealousy raged within her heart. She hated to think that he might have been unfaithful to her but what else could lie behind the triumphant gleam she was sure had glistened in Caroline's eyes. Perhaps his suggestion of a separation had its root in his guilt. Was it the beginnings of a final end to their marriage? Judith pressed her hot cheek against the cool pillow, suppressing the weak tears, urging herself to fight for her marriage. But was there anything left to fight for? She had felt in her heart on the day she was married that it was all a mistake and events had proved her right. She recalled the sadness that had possessed her then and now she understood it for surely she had known that marriage to Mark would not bring happiness. It was far better to give in gracefully to his suggestion and let Caroline have him—perhaps they were better suited, after all.

But she could not rid herself of the feeling that Mark had suffered too during the past weeks. There had been an urgency in his arms, desperation in the seeking of his lips, and a strain in his voice that she had never known before. She had felt that she mattered to him and that he needed her beyond either his or her imaginings. Unless he had been only trying to atone for his feelings of guilt...

No, it was too late, much too late, and they could never make anything of their marriage now. Too much water had passed under the bridge. Lying in the cool darkness, with tears on her cheeks, she sadly made her plans. She would leave the Lodge the very next day and go to her father's house for a little while. They would have to know that she and Mark had parted and a natural pride made her shrink from the ordeal but she was sure her father would be sympathetic and understanding.

It was a sorry end to all her hopes and dreams...

After a sleepless night, the thought of eating appalled her and she pushed away untouched the attractive breakfast tray which Sarah brought up to her room, heedless of that good person's protests. She had long since won over Alexander and Sarah and between themselves they discussed the disturbing events which were taking place and worried over the master and his wife.

Judith tried to doze but her brain was too active and her heart too full. She rose late and dressed with little interest in the clothes she decided to wear for the journey to Pelham.

With care born only of habit, she dressed her golden hair into its neat chignon and listlessly applied her make-up. When she went down to the lounge, Digger ran forward to greet her. He was exuberant and affectionate as always when Mark was not available to receive his lavish demonstrations. His pink, wet tongue licked Judith's fingers as she bent to caress him, he sighed gustily and wagged his tail energetically. Judith was the second person in Digger's life and he was devoted to her. She fondled his ears absently and then sat down to toy with the coffee that Alexander brought her with a solicitous inquiry about her health and a comforting remark on the weather. He also informed her that David Ancell had already telephoned to inquire after Casey.

Judith picked up her letters and idly glanced through them. There was little to interest her among them and she put them aside indifferently after only a cursory glance. Her head was aching dully and her heart was sick with the sense of loss and the renewed unhappiness.

What would happen next? she wondered. Presumably a letter from Mark's lawyers full of legal jargon. The discussion of money settlements and separation pending divorce—divorce so that he could marry

Caroline? The very thought struck her anew with swift pain and jealousy. She sighed. She had hoped for so much from her marriage and it had been to no avail despite her determination to win Mark's love and make a success of their life together.

The sun streamed in through the windows of the lounge. It was a glorious morning with blue skies, a mere wisp of white cloud scudding overhead, warm sunshine and the light-hearted song of the birds in the trees which surrounded the Lodge. The sunshine touched the glistening dew on the emerald green of the lawns.

Judith walked across to the windows and threw them wide. For a long time she stood there, listening to the birds, absorbing the warmth and wondering how she could bear to leave the place she loved so much. She had readily given her heart to Mark's home. Now summer was fast bringing its glories to Hurleigh. But she knew she could not stay while memories crowded about her. The sun only enhanced her misery and she turned away.

She packed a few things, having telephoned the station to check on the train times. Most of her clothes and other possessions could be sent on when she had decided what to do with her life. She could not stay at Pelham indefinitely and she supposed that a flat in London would eventually solve her problems.

There were no more tears now. She felt a strange numbness take possession of her and she knew that no matter what it cost her she could go through with this separation that Mark wanted. Far better to break the ties which bound them than to suffer any longer the bitter unhappiness of the past few months. It did not matter now that she had been wrongly accused—if Mark had loved her he would never have thought so ill of her and she wanted no more of a marriage in which love was so one-sided.

When Mark telephoned, she could be

cool and casual and seemingly indifferent though the tears pricked her eyelids. Bitterly, she told herself when she turned away from the telephone that her decision meant nothing to Mark. No doubt he was relieved that she was being sensible, admitting that this was the end...

Clifford Shaw said little when his daughter arrived at his house. Since their week-end at the Lodge, he had been disturbed and anxious about Judith, sure that all was not well with her marriage. So he greeted her warmly, made no mention of Mark and waited patiently for her explanations. They were not long in coming for Judith had always loved and confided in her father and was sure of his understanding. He listened in silence to the recital of her unhappiness, her conviction that she had been mistaken in marrying Mark and their decision to separate.

At last he said soberly: 'Well, you're not a fool, Judith, and I dare say you've talked this over with Mark. If you both feel it's futile to try again, then it's better that you part. You're welcome to stay with us, my dear. Mary is fond of you and will understand.'

She shook her head. 'I only want to stay for a few days, Daddy. Then I must try to find a flat in Town and pick up the old threads again.' A dry little laugh escaped her. 'It shouldn't be very difficult as I've only been out of circulation a few months.'

'Have you thought about your future?' Clifford asked. 'What do you intend to do?'

She shrugged. 'I haven't made up my mind yet. Oh, there'll be plenty of ways to pass the time, I expect.'

'Mark will arrange a settlement, of course.'

'There's been little time to discuss that sort of thing,' she returned. 'But there's always Mother's money—and perhaps I'll get a job. Debbie Baxter always wanted me to be a partner in her dress shop. That might be quite interesting.'

The house which Clifford Shaw had bought on his second marriage was small but pleasant. The atmosphere was one of quiet contentment despite the ring of childish voices about the house. Judith settled in quickly, finding some consolation mingled with sadness in the company of the two children and the even placidity and kindness of her young stepmother. Mary was too tactful to ply the girl with questions and had no thought of condemnation because her marriage had failed. Instead, she did her best to make Judith feel welcome, found several little tasks to while away the days and encouraged her interest in the children.

Judith found herself reluctant to leave Pelham and her father pressed her to stay longer so more than a week passed and still she had made no effort to find a flat in London. She heard nothing from Mark and did not contact him, trying to forget her unhappiness in new pleasures and the childish affection of Mandy and Michael who quickly attached themselves to her and made their devotion obvious. She wrote to Casey, avoiding all mention of the separation for she did not know if Mark would have told the young man, merely letting him know that she was staying with her father for a few days but would be in London very soon.

Mark did not tell Caroline Mallow what had happened but he felt that she knew for he never mentioned Judith and had not returned to Hurleigh since the night of Casey's accident. He continued to sleep at the Club and Caroline was content to enjoy the amenities of his flat for she loved London life and the gay social round. They saw each other frequently and she was not blind to his grim mood. Anxiety for his one-time ward could explain it but Caroline was shrewd enough to know that it went much deeper. He was always pleasant and charming to her but dull anger smouldered beneath the façade and she waited patiently for him to confide in her. They had not been friends all these years for nothing and Caroline's love for Mark made her sensitive. A thrill of triumph was in her blood for she was sure that all was over between him and Judith. Caroline was determined to win Mark for herself and she was not over-scrupulous about her methods.

One evening he let himself in to the flat as she was adding last-minute touches to her make-up before leaving for a dinner engagement. She came out of the bedroom and went into the lounge to find him sprawled in an armchair, long legs stretched out, a hand over his closed eyes.

Without a word, she helped herself to a cigarette from the filigree box on the low table. He opened his eyes and glanced at her. 'Going out?' he asked.

She nodded. 'Rather a bore,' she replied easily. 'I'm dining with the Nelsons.' She made a little moué.

'Why bother?' he asked.

Caroline shrugged. 'It's a long-standing engagement,' she murmured, exhaling blue-grey smoke which wreathed about her auburn head.

'So you're deserting your Italian admirer?'

'Guilio? Oh, it won't break his heart,' she laughed.

Mark studied her through half-closed eyes. She was looking extremely beautiful, her hair gleaming in the light, coquetry in her green eyes and a black velvet evening gown embracing her superb figure. Her flawless skin did not betray her thirty-odd years and she wore an air of mature sophistication which attracted Mark in that moment. With a flicker of surprise, he realized that he had never regarded her as a beautiful woman before. One of the disadvantages of knowing a woman too well—he had lost count of the many years they had been friends.

'Why not dine with me?' he asked abruptly.

She smiled. 'It would be pleasant,' she said and then demurred: 'But I'd better not disappoint the Nelsons.'

He rose to his feet. 'I wish you would,' he said. 'I'm at a loose end—and I'm in such a confounded mood tonight that I can't bear my own company.'

Caroline thought for a moment, looking up into his handsome face, noting the tiny signs of strain about his eyes and the tautness of his mouth. Then she nodded. 'All right, Mark—go and change while I telephone Louise and make my apologies.'

They dined at a small, intimate night-club and in its atmosphere, Mark seemed to relax. Caroline was good company and sensitive to his mood, talking little, sobering her natural gaiety, making every effort to make her charms felt in the most subtle way. They danced, and Mark was very conscious of the trace of perfume she wore, the nearness of her slim body and eager response in her movements. As they moved about the small crowded floor to the rhythmic music of the excellent orchestra, he thought of the many times they had danced together in the past, the many times he had enjoyed her company and found her amusing, the bond of friendship which held them. He knew that Caroline had loved him for years—or imagined that she did. He knew also that she had hoped to marry him eventually and his own inner sadness brought a swift sympathy for Caroline's vain hopes. Wryly, he wondered if he should not have married her years ago and if they would have found happiness together. But he had never loved her and Mark realized only too well that in marrying Judith without loving her he had made a great mistake.

It had not been enough that he was fond of her, that he enjoyed her company and appreciated her worth or that she loved him. They had made a sorry beginning to the material of marriage which needed such careful weaving. He loved her deeply now but he had failed her terribly by his initial lack of love and Mark felt sure that it had been his coldness, his inability to love in return which had driven her to deceit and disloyalty. She was a warm-hearted person and she needed the response of warmth from the man she had married. Her saw this all too clearly now that it was too late. In her decision to leave Hurleigh and her agreement to a separation, Mark read a realization that she had given up all hope of saving their marriage.

They resumed their seats and Mark poured fresh wine into their glasses. Caroline raised her glass to him with a smile. 'To the future, Mark!'

Dryly he replied: 'What future? A gloomy one lies ahead of me, I'm afraid.'

She leaned forward quickly. 'Why, Mark? What's wrong?'

He shrugged. 'Everything at the moment.

The Van Doren deal didn't work out—I'm worried about Casey...'

'How is he now?' Caroline asked eagerly.

'He seems well enough—but he won't believe that anything serious is wrong and he's impatient at being kept in the nursing home. Unfortunately, Keiller isn't so happy about his condition. He doesn't say much—won't commit himself, I suppose, but he shakes his head and looks anxious and mutters about more x-rays.'

'Poor old Casey!' Caroline murmured sympathetically. 'I must go and see him tomorrow.' She laid a gentle hand on Mark's arm. 'But that isn't all that's troubling you, is it, my dear?' she asked quietly.

He met her eyes and the warm sympathy in their depths invited his confidence. Slowly, he said: 'No, it isn't Caroline. Judith and I have parted—we decided to call it a day!'

This was even more than Caroline had hoped for but she carefully concealed the thrill of triumph. 'My poor Mark,' she said gently. 'I'm so sorry.'

He shrugged. 'It's one of those things,' he returned curtly. 'It wasn't a success—far better to end it now than let things drag on hopelessly.'

Wisely, Caroline said no more but endeavoured to convey human sympathy in her eyes and demeanour for the rest of the evening. When he escorted her back to the flat he refused the offer of coffee and very soon murmured something about getting to the Club.

She glanced at her watch. 'You could stay here, Mark,' she said, deliberately casual. Her tone gave nothing away but the look she flashed at him offered a provocative invitation for Caroline was in the mood to stop at nothing which would end his marriage once and for all.

Mark hesitated. He was not blind to the invitation and he had been conscious all evening of her attractions. Bitterly he reminded himself that all was over between

him and Judith and she would not care
where he spent his nights in future. Since
his marriage, he had gradually come to
regard Caroline as a woman and the
brotherly attitude he had once adopted
seemed out of place now they were both
mature adults.

Sensing his hesitation, Caroline said
easily: 'I'm not worried about convention,
Mark darling. I'm not ashamed to admit
that I'm in love with you.'

He gave an impatient gesture. 'Don't
let's talk of love, Caroline. If I stayed
here with you, love wouldn't come into it
where I'm concerned.' He was deliberately
brutal and she flushed slightly. But she
went quickly to his side and laid a hand
on his arm.

'I don't care,' she said quickly. 'I love
you—and I want you on any terms.'

He looked down at her. 'At least you're
honest,' he said. His lips twisted. 'You've
never lied to me, Caroline.'

'Because I'm not ashamed of any of my

actions,' she said impulsively. She met his eyes and he looked into the green depths and felt his senses swim slightly. But then he thought of Judith and her fair innocence—the pure line of her proud chin was before his eyes and the sweetness of her expression.

He shook his head. 'No, I won't stay, Caro.' He used the old familiar nickname to soften his decision for he knew she would be naturally angry that he scorned her warm invitation.

When he had gone, Caroline stared at the closed door with anger openly gleaming in her green eyes. She stubbed her cigarette viciously for she longed for his arms and the heat of his passion. This was the final rebuff and she made up her mind that she had wasted enough time on Mark Debenham.

On the way to the Club, Mark told himself that he had done the wisest thing. If it came about that Judith had discovered his indiscretion, she would despise him for being guilty of the same fault for which he had condemned and punished her. Because he loved her, he was thankful that he had refuted temptation. Thinking along these lines and remembering that Judith had loved him without a shadow of a doubt, he began to wonder if he had accused her wrongly.

It was easy to misconstrue an innocent action and easier still for a man with a hasty temper like his to leap to conclusions and judge harshly. He remembered that after the first brazen outburst, Judith had been insistent in protesting her innocence. He now blamed himself for denying her a chance to explain and knew his temper and jealousy to be responsible. He had feared that his suspicions would be proved...

At the time, it had seemed incredible that his sweet and honest Judith could be capable of such disloyalty. Now he mused over the matter with an open mind and felt almost convinced that he had misjudged her. But it was too late now to seek her out for the truth. If she were innocent, then his behaviour must have broken her heart in reality and could the delicate flower of love survive such cruel treatment? Was it because she no longer loved him that she accepted the dictum of a separation and made his path easier by leaving the home they had shared?

He had no answer to his questions but still they seethed through his brain and his heart was heavy when he admitted that he had probably lost the wife he loved through his own blind and harsh injustice.

CHAPTER X

Casey's pleasure at sight of Judith was something that she carried with her for a long time. He stretched out a hand to her but the movement was weak and pity swept through her when she realized what an effort it had cost him. She hurried to his side and, bending over him, pressed her lips to his cheek, compassionate, warmly affectionate. Then, carrying off the emotional moment, she lightly kissed the tip of his nose. He smiled up at her at the gesture.

'I'm surprised to see you still lying here,' she told him lightly. 'I thought you'd be up and chasing your pretty nurses by now.'

His eyes were on her face and there was a light in their depths which spoke of the hunger he had felt to see her, to hear her voice and to have her near to him.

'There aren't any as pretty as you,' he replied, 'so it isn't enough incentive.'

She sat down in the comfortable chair beside the bed and peeled off the thin white gloves she wore. 'Does Sir Martin tell you how you're progressing, Casey?' she asked, keeping all trace of anxiety from her voice.

'He tells me nothing,' was the harsh retort. 'I don't think he knows much himself despite his great reputation. All I hear from him and my nurse is an injunction to be patient.' A broad smile lit his face. 'Can you imagine me being patient, Judy?'

She smiled. 'It must be difficult—but I'm sure it won't be for long! Sir Martin's such a clever man...'

'So he may be,' interrupted Casey. 'But my case seems to baffle him.' The days of immobility had caused his cheerfulness to wear thin and there were tell-tale signs of anxiety about his blue-grey eyes and the thin, sensitive mouth. 'He's hoping to interest a German specialist in me,' he added but there was a note of hopelessness in his voice. A moment later he spoke rather more brightly: 'Tell me how you are, Judy? I've been longing to see you ever since I had your letter. Mark's been in every day and Caroline's been to see me—but it was you I wanted to see.'

She dropped her eyes at mention of Mark. She had left Pelham two days ago. Debbie Baxter had offered her a job at the dress shop and invited her to share the flat she rented in return to a letter which Judith wrote to her. Debbie was a modern young woman with little respect for marriage and the news that Judith had left her husband seemed to surprise her not at all. Judith had known a strange reluctance to leave the peaceful security of Pelham and her father's home but she knew that now was the time to prove her independence and an ability to run her own life.

'I'm sorry I haven't been sooner, Casey

—but I've been having a restful stay at Pelham and now I feel like a new woman.'

Casey studied her closely. She had a little colour and some of the strain had left her eyes. Perhaps she had reconciled herself to the end of her life with Mark. 'If it's a sore subject, we won't discuss you and Mark,' he said quietly, 'but I'd like to say that I'm very upset over your decision to separate.'

She toyed with her gloves. 'So am I,' she said in a low voice. 'But Mark suggested it and we couldn't go on as we were. I had to agree, Casey.' She added bitterly: 'Even I had to admit that it was a mistake from the start.'

Casey looked sober. 'Were things that bad between you two? Couldn't you have patched up your marriage one day?'

She shrugged listlessly. 'Let's face it, Casey—never were two people more un-suited for marriage than Mark and I.'

Casey's chin took on a stubborn lift.

'I don't agree with you,' he said firmly. 'I don't think that either of you had a chance to find happiness—Mark was much too quick to condemn you...' He stopped abruptly. Too late for a dawning flush tinged Judith's cheeks.

'So Mark told you,' she said slowly. She felt a rising anger that her husband should discuss such a personal matter even with so close a friend as Casey. She looked towards the window. 'I often thought you knew,' she said quietly, 'but I'm surprised that Mark should take you into his confidence when I remember all he said about it when I wanted your help and advice.' Her voice was bitter. She turned to look at him. 'I suppose you too have condemned me? It's too much to hope that Mark wouldn't impress on you the enormity of my guilt. He wasted no time in assuming that I couldn't possibly be innocent!'

'Judith.' He said her name gently and she met his eyes levelly. 'I've never believed what Mark said of you,' he assured her sincerely. 'I told him at the time that I'd never heard such a cock-and-bull story in my life. I know you well enough, Judith, to believe completely in your innocence—and I'm well aware that you've always been deeply in love with Mark.'

Tears sprang to her eyes and in a voice choked with emotion, she told him the true story, not whitening her own deceitful part in it nor denying that she had at first reacted to Mark's accusation with brazen defiance.

He listened in silence, glad that he had doubted Mark's version, relieved at her innocence and yet angry that she had not tried harder to clear herself of such a black smear against her integrity. But he said nothing of his natural anger, only determining that Mark should know the truth and confident that if Mark were to investigate Judith's account of that night all shadow of doubt would be removed. It was evident that Judith was unhappy and no more wanted this stupid separation than did Mark—for Casey was not easily deceived and he knew that nothing but pride had led Mark to take such a step. Casey was convinced that soon the two people who mattered so much to him could be brought together again and all that was needed to ensure their happiness was mutual love and understanding.

Because it was easy to talk to Casey, Judith mentioned her fears that Caroline was trying to wean Mark completely from his marriage.

Casey scoffed at this. 'Mark has known her too long and too well, my dear,' he assured her. 'If it was meant that there should be anything between them, it would have happened long ago. Don't worry, Judith. Mark isn't likely to find consolation in any woman's arms, let alone Caroline's!' His confidence reassured her a little but she could not explain the deep-rooted and age-old suspicion of the woman she thought of as a rival to Mark's affections. They spoke of other things and Casey made an effort to seem gay and light-hearted. When his young nurse came into the room she was glad to see his handsome face alight with eager animation.

Judith rose to her feet, realizing that her visit must come to an end. She picked up her gloves and handbag. 'I must go now, Casey,' she said gently. 'But I'll come again very soon now that I'm living in London.' She bent to bestow a brief kiss on Casey's cheek, smiled warmly at the nurse who waited patiently by the window and then left the room.

Ann Davenport came to the bed. 'I'm afraid you must prepare yourself for an intensive examination, my boy. Dr Kahn agreed to have a look at your back and he's with Sir Martin now.'

Casey groaned. 'This is where the whole damn rigmarole starts again!' he prophesied. 'Poking and prodding and dozens of questions.'

'You're very lucky that Dr Kahn happens

to be in England,' Ann told him firmly. 'He's very brilliant and if anyone can give a definite verdict, then he can!'

'I don't care what the verdict is,' he grumbled, 'as long as I can leave this place and go back to Hurleigh.' Suddenly he smiled up at her. 'I think you're the only person who keeps me sane, Ann girl!'

The girl returned his smile and Casey noted again her open, friendly countenance, the sweet mouth and the bright merry eyes.

Casey was not fickle but he had resigned himself to the knowledge that Judith was not for him and never could be. He had known a restlessness, a vague sense that something was lacking, and a longing for a stable and worthwhile anchor in his life. Since he had met Ann Davenport and known her sweetness and the innate kindness, he was beginning to wonder if a girl like this one might not in time assuage his nameless need. She was a person with great warmth and a very human sympathy: she possessed a fund of cheerfulness and understanding which he appreciated. He enjoyed her company and would be glad of the opportunity to know her outside the starched and professional world of medicine. She was young and responded swiftly to Casey's own youth: she was gentle with him, cheerful, friendly and very likeable; he was beginning to depend on her and knew that he would miss her when he left the nursing-home. He was a warm-hearted young man and he had already grown fond of his pretty nurse.

Now, as she made him comfortable, smoothed his pillows and gave him a drink to moisten the dry lips, she said easily: 'What an attractive woman? Is she your best girl, Casey?'

He grinned. 'Not on your life! She's married to my one-time guardian.' A slight cloud marred his face as he remembered that the marriage was not a success. But then he added mischievously: 'Why? Does a spark of jealousy burn beneath that white apron, Ann girl?'

She tidied the locker beside his bed. If he had disturbed her composure, she gave no sign of it. 'I haven't a jealous bone in my body,' she told him with a light laugh.

He regarded her curiously. 'Are you engaged or anything, Ann?' he asked. 'I know so little about you.'

She glanced at him. 'Is there any reason why you should know more?'

'I'm interested,' he retorted.

She paused a moment. Then she said: 'No, I'm not engaged or anything.'

He sighed. 'I dare say you have dozens of dates—a pretty girl like you. There can't be many men who'd pass up the opportunity to take you out.'

'Compliments to the nurses are forbidden,' she told him with mock severity as a smile played about her mouth.

'What do you think this German chap will make of me?' he asked, going off at a tangent. His anxiety about his injured back could not stay hidden for long.

She folded her arms and looked down at him. 'I don't know,' she said slowly. 'I wish I could tell you.'

'What happens if he says I'm doomed to be on my back for the rest of my life?' he demanded.

'Sir Martin will send you home,' Ann said. 'With a private nurse, of course. You'll be much better off in the country—and you've told me so much about your lovely home, I'm sure you'll be glad to leave this "dump", as you call it.'

'It is a lovely home,' he assured her. 'Set in beautiful surroundings.' He sighed again. 'You'd love it, Ann girl,' he assured her. 'Couldn't you come and nurse me? We'd be able to go for lovely walks together—if you're strong enough to push a wheelchair up and down the hills!' he added bitterly.

Ann smiled and with a gentle hand brushed back the unruly hair which fell across the sensitive brow and made him look so boyish and appealing. 'We'll see,' she said. 'I wouldn't mind the job. I love the country and walking is one of my favourite pastimes.' She added tenderly: 'Let's hope you won't need the wheelchair, Casey—and if you go home well, then I'll come down to see you and you can walk with me up and down those beloved hills of yours!' With a laugh, she then said: 'If you want it that way, of course.'

He nodded. 'Yes, I do, Ann girl. I want very much to see you again once I leave this place. You will come—Promise?' He was sincere and there was pleading in his eyes and voice.

'Let's wait and see what happens, shall we?'

And he had to be content with this for the time being. He fell silent and waited for the two doctors to come. Ann continued to tidy the room and she glanced in his direction once or twice as though sensing the inner turmoil which now seized him.

Sir Martin's despondency and reluctance to commit himself definitely had not failed to impress the young man with the gravity of his unlucky fall. Despite his general light-hearted scorn and the repeated prophecy that he would be well in no time, Casey was very worried. Inactivity did not rest easily on his shoulders and the thoughts of a future in which he was helpless as he had been these past two weeks threw a shadow over his gaiety and confidence. At last, steps were heard in the corridor and the voices of the two men reached Casey's ears.

Swiftly, Ann sped to the bedside, leaned down to brush her lips across his brow and murmured: 'Bear up, my boy! It might be bad news but I know you can take it.'

He gave her a grateful smile as the door opened and she was instantly professional again. Sir Martin introduced his German colleague who smiled reassuringly down at the young man. The examination was long and detailed and the doctors frequently referred to the x-rays which they had brought with them.

Kahn was gentle but capable and the sensitive fingers touched and probed and pressed. Casey felt a conviction that the German was not only interested but also brilliantly able. Once or twice, Casey winced at a shaft of pain. It was the first time he had experienced pain in his back and when he told Kahn this, the German nodded soberly.

'Ach so! So it hurts when I press here ... and perhaps here, does it?'

'Yes, that's right.'

The German grunted. He turned to Keiller, saying something in a low tone which Casey did not hear. Sir Martin nodded, as if in agreement, then he too touched the same spot on Casey's spine. His legs jumped involuntarily.

Kahn moved away from the bed and indicated that Keiller should follow him. They stood by the window, holding x-ray photographs to the light, talking in low voices. At one point, the German made a sharp exclamation and indicated a certain part of the spine to Keiller. Then he turned back to the bed and said: 'This is going to hurt, young man—perhaps very much. But I do nothing without good reason.' As he spoke, his hands were again on Casey's back.

Casey never knew what the specialist did with his long, slim and clever hands for pain suddenly flooded him to such extent that he lost consciousness. Kahn was able to manipulate and manoeuvre until he was satisfied that he could do no more.

Then he straightened up with a confident gleam in his eyes. 'Quite remarkable!' he commented. 'But very possible with such a fall as you described.' He smiled compassionately down at the unconscious Casey. 'A few weeks of pain for this one—then gradually returning strength and activity.'

'You've had experience of this kind of case in Germany?' Sir Martin asked with live interest. Only time would prove if Kahn's treatment was successful but the German's confidence was impressive.

'Once in Vienna—some years ago,' Kahn replied. 'There was a similarity in the x-rays which reminded me. Such a small thing which can be easily overlooked and might mean paralysis for an indefinite period.'

When Casey recovered consciousness, Ann stood by the bed, her eyes shining happily, a hypodermic needle in her hand. He was hardly conscious of her presence for severe pain possessed him completely. Sympathy flashed into her eyes as she said gently: 'We can't help with the pain, my boy, but I'm going to give you an injection to dull it for you. Comfort yourself with the knowledge that you're going to be all right.'

Hope was in his eyes as he looked up at her, the words reaching him vaguely through the waves of pain. 'Is that a fact?' he murmured.

'Well, we hope so,' she said. 'Dr Kahn is very pleased with himself and I think that must be a good sign.'

He grinned feebly and then his lips twisted with pain. 'What the hell have they done to me?' he managed to force between stiff lips.

'Nothing but good, Casey—believe that. In some cases, pain is a healing process.'

'Cold comfort!' A trace of a smile was in his eyes as she bent over him with the hypodermic and the last thing he remembered for some time was the clear smoothness of her skin and the length of the dark lashes surrounding the warm brown of her eyes.

Judith took a taxi back to the flat she was now sharing with Debbie. She leaned against the cold leather seat, idly scanning the crowds in the London streets, thinking of Casey and, reluctantly of Mark. Why had there been no letter from his lawyers? Was he hesitating to draw up a legal separation? Or was it merely that he was too busy to attend to such a trivial detail in his life? Her lips twisted bitterly. She had always been a mere detail to him, she told herself—so many things had been placed before her that it was not surprising their life together had been a disappointing failure. Resentfully, she thought of the business ties which had caused him to leave her so much alone in Paris—easy prey for a charming, soft-spoken and attractive Perry Congrieve.

Bond Street—and the taxi halted for traffic lights. Instinctively, Judith leaned forward to catch sight of the white façade of the Debenham Galleries and there was a faint hope in her heart that she might catch a glimpse of Mark. Faint hope but it was granted for just then his tall figure appeared through the seething crowd as he came out of the Galleries. Her heart leaped with a sickening movement at sight of that proud, dark head, the broad shoulders and easy, lithe movement as he walked briskly towards her taxi. In a moment, she made up her mind. She got out, paid off the surprised driver and turned to walk towards Mark. Colour was in her cheeks and her heart beat fast and alarmingly.

Mark stopped with surprise as the slim, well-known figure of his wife drew near. She was looking very well, he thought, and very chic in the flame-coloured suit with white accessories. His heart was in turmoil at sight of her. Was she coming in search of him—or was their meeting a mere coincidence? If the first was the right answer was it an olive branch—an opportunity to mend their differences... He had no time for further conjecture for she reached him.

At the last moment, Judith had known a strong desire to turn and run for she was afraid of her reception—and certainly the grim expression of the man who waited for her was not reassuring.

'Hallo, Judith,' he said in stilted tones. 'This is a surprise meeting.'

'Hallo, Mark. I was coming down Bond

Street in a taxi when I saw you leave the Galleries.' She looked about her at the milling passers-by. 'There's such a lot to discuss, Mark,' she said, stumbling on the words. 'I thought it best to catch you now...' She broke off for a grin spread over his face.

'Catching the bull by the horns, Judith?' he asked. He took her arm. 'Come and have coffee with me,' he invited, 'then we can do all the necessary talking.' He gestured around them. 'This is impossible.'

She stirred her coffee idly and then toyed with her spoon nervously. Mark sat watching her and his eyes held an enigmatic expression.

'I thought I would hear from you by now,' she said at last, slowly. 'But I suppose the progress of law is very slow.'

He brought out his cigarette case. 'I haven't spoken to Lesser yet.'

She flashed him a surprised glance. 'No? But surely...' she stopped.

He shrugged and offered the cigarettes.

'Is there any particular hurry? Does it matter if we make it legal? As far as we're concerned, we're living apart, my dear—isn't that enough?' His eyes narrowed. 'Unless, of course, you're worried about a settlement...'

'No,' she said quickly. 'I don't want your money, Mark—I have my own and I've been offered a good job. I'd rather not take money from you.'

'That's a ridiculous attitude,' he told her with a slight sharpness in his voice. 'After all, you're still my wife and I intend to support you.' He exhaled cigarette smoke with a sudden harsh breath. 'How was your father?' he asked politely.

For a few moments they discussed Pelham and Clifford Shaw: they went on to talk of Casey and gradually Judith's sense of embarrassment at being with Mark like this faded. A wry smile touched her lips and Mark raised an interrogative eyebrow.

She said slowly: 'It just occurred to me—I suppose we're being very "modern" about all this. I hardly expected to be drinking coffee with you this morning and casually talking of this and that.'

He leaned forward. 'We used to be very good friends once, Judith,' he said quietly. 'Because we failed to live together amicably as husband and wife, does that mean the end of our friendship?'

She drew a sharp breath. 'Mark, modern or not, I don't like it. You once told me that you were old-fashioned about marriage? How can you reconcile those views with separation from your wife?'

He leaned forward and there was an eager light in his eyes. 'Judith, are you regretting it?'

She looked down at her hands and then she said: 'It isn't easy for me to think of our marriage as ended, Mark.' She looked up and caught her breath sharply at the look in his eyes. He placed a hand over her tense fingers and was about to speak when she looked over his shoulder and her eyes hardened. He turned to see Caroline Mallow threading her way through the tables towards them. Her easy confidence and sophisticated beauty struck Judith forcibly and she withdrew her fingers from Mark's grasp.

'Mark!' Caroline exclaimed warmly. 'Am I terribly late?'

He glanced at his watch. 'Not more than usual.'

Caroline turned to Judith with a dazzling smile. 'This is an unexpected pleasure. How are you, darling? Mark!' she accused, 'you didn't tell me that we were to be a threesome.'

Judith searched Mark's face with anguish in her eyes. She had been ready to pocket her pride, to beg Mark for a reconciliation but now she was angry at Caroline's arrival, obviously by arrangement with Mark.

Mark looked up at Caroline and said smoothly: 'I'd forgotten we arranged to meet here, Caro—bumping into Judith in Bond Street drove it out of my head.' If he was embarrassed by the situation it was not evident in voice or demeanour. 'Sit down, Caro...' he invited.

'Please do,' Judith said sweetly. 'I was just leaving anyway.' She flashed Mark a cool glance and received a vaguely-apologetic shrug of the shoulders. 'Mark and I have said all there is to say,' she added evenly. As she rose, she said to Mark with icy anger: 'I think it would be better if you do contact Lesser. I'm not very pleased with the present situation—and if you don't do something soon, then I will.' She gave Caroline a meaning glance.

Caroline sat back, smiling to herself as she listened to Judith's barely-controlled anger which sparked in her words. Mark rose politely as Judith turned on her heel and stalked from the restaurant. Then he threw himself down into his chair again and cursed softly under his breath.

'I gather I arrived at an inopportune moment,' Caroline said smoothly. 'Judith wasn't very pleased—you really should have told her about our appointment, Mark.'

'I forgot,' he muttered.

Caroline helped herself to a cigarette from the case which lay in front of him. 'Oh well, she's much too sensible to suspect that there's anything clandestine in our meeting. She's looking very well and much happier,' she added lightly.

Mark flashed her a sharp glance. 'Do you really think she's happier?' he demanded for he had received an entirely different impression.

Caroline flicked her lighter into life and bent her head over the flame. 'A woman can always sense these things, Mark darling. I think her pride is hurt, which is natural—but she's relieved and thankful that you've parted now the actual step has been taken.' She glanced at him obliquely. 'No slur on you, darling, but she was never happy at Hurleigh.' He moved impatiently but before he could speak, she went on: 'Think it over, Mark—and you must agree with me that you and Judith never had enough in common to make a success of marriage.' She was wise enough to say no more on the subject and she went on to talk of the circumstances which had brought about their meeting that morning. One of her Italian friends was interested in buying a painting which had been offered to him by a private dealer. Caroline had asked Mark to have a look at the painting and give his opinion of its value for she felt that the sale price was exorbitant.

Mark went down to Hurleigh that night. For the first time since he left the Lodge to return to Town, he knew a longing to be back in the home he loved. In his heart he knew that his former reluctance was due to Judith's absence but he must get used to the idea that she had gone out of his life. In a few short months, she had made her presence felt at the Lodge, giving an atmosphere to the house which had been lacking until she came to it as Mark's bride. On the way to the village, he thought longingly of relaxation in familiar surroundings, the faithful devotion of Digger, the sensed but unspoken loyalty of Alexander and Sarah. He thought wryly that they would be speculating on Judith's sudden departure and wondering if she would ever return for they were shrewd and far-seeing and neither Mark nor Judith had made a secret of their differences. There had been more truth in Caroline's words than he cared to admit. Judith had never been happy at Hurleigh—from the beginning he had failed her and the ensuing misunderstandings between them had brought fresh and bitter unhappiness. They were both to blame. Whether the fault lay more on one side than the other seemed immaterial now. He remembered her words that morning: *'It isn't easy for me to think of our marriage as ended.'* Could he take that as proof that in her eyes it definitely was ended? Or had that been his cue to suggest a second trial? Why the devil had he forgotten his appointment with Caroline? And what had possessed him to suggest that particular restaurant for morning coffee? Judith had been justifiably angry at Caroline's arrival and Mark realized with a frown that the woman had greeted him with a warm possessiveness. To be sure, she had always spoken to him in such a manner for she had the privilege of long friendship. Mark had certainly given it little thought but Judith's expression had stirred in him a faint resentment that Caroline's greeting should be so affectionate.

Was there a motive in the woman's actions? She was being particularly charming of late, seeming to seek his company and his eyes narrowed as he remembered her blatant declaration of love and the invitation she had offered. Was it possible that Caroline still hoped...? He brushed the thought aside but it persisted during the drive. Mark had known only too well that Caroline cared for him: her jealous anger on his marriage had been obvious to the man who knew her every mood; was it possible that his separation pleased her and renewed hope in her heart of an opportunity to take Judith's place? Gradually he realized that the idea was not so ridiculous as it had first seemed.

Alexander greeted him with his usual austere deference and inquired if Mrs Debenham was to be expected shortly in a tone which skilfully covered any speculative wonder on his part. Curtly Mark informed him that his wife was staying in London for the present and strode into the lounge. At the familiar step, Digger threw himself at Mark, his barked excitement mingled with reproach at his long absence. Casually Mark rubbed his ears to atone for his neglect.

The house seemed strangely empty: not only because of Judith's absence but also because Casey lay in bed at the London nursing-home and Mark missed his gay and youthful exuberance, the knowledge that he was somewhere about the house or grounds.

The day brought warm summer sunshine and an azure blue sky. Mark rose early and ate breakfast alone but for Digger who trotted in and out of the room through the open french windows, holding up a paw to Mark, reminding him that it was an ideal day for a long tramp over the fields and a long time since they had indulged in such pleasurable pastime. Mark read all this in the dog's pleading brown eyes, rubbed his ears with a swift caress and promised him the desired tramp later. At this, Digger raced out into the garden and back again, hurtling himself against Mark's feet in rapturous abandonment. Digger could not understand why it wasn't always summer and in the winter, lying by the fire or confined to the house because of the inclement weather, he harboured a grudge against the season which, however, was instantly forgotten at the first sight of the sun which heralds the summer.

The glorious day also brought good news which eased a little of the pain in Mark's heart. Casey would in time be as fit and active as ever he had been—it was merely the time factor now that mattered.

But pain lived with him still for the loss of Judith. He loved her so dearly and no amount of time would alter that fact. Pain flowed over him at the thought of her—it was a pain he would know more intimately in the future, he told himself, for time would not ease the bitter loneliness, the sense of loss, the longing to have her near him and to know the happiness which he felt could be theirs if only they had the chance.

He walked for hours with Digger running ahead or trotting obediently at his heels. He was barely conscious of his surroundings for he thought of Judith. When he finally turned his steps homeward, he was a determined man for he knew that he loved Judith too much to live without her. If there were any way to regain the precious gift of her love, then he would find it: he was prepared to fight every inch of the way for happiness with the woman he was proud to call his wife. The tide of loneliness had washed away all bitter doubts where her loyalty was concerned and he knew that when she was once again in his arms, there would be no question of forgiveness.

CHAPTER XI

Mark turned from the bar at the sound of his own name. He was enjoying a drink with an old friend during a brief lull in his busy day for he was once again in London. The club was not unduly full but Mark was well-known and had several friends among the members. He turned, expecting to greet an acquaintance.

A tall fair man was talking with the Club Secretary. Mark scrutinized the stranger and then turned back to his friend but some minutes later, the Secretary touched his arm. 'Mark, old chap—may I introduce Perry Congrieve, an old friend of mine.'

Mark tensed at the name but his manners and breeding did not fail. He shook hands with the young man and ordered drinks for them all. While they waited for the drinks, he studied Congrieve under cover of casual conversation. Was this in fact the man that Judith had met in Paris? Fair, good-looking, a little Continental in dress and mannerisms, pleasant, charming and young—his eyes narrowed as he thought that these were all things which might attract Judith.

The Secretary was called away to his office and Mark's friend soon excused himself on the plea of an appointment. Mark and Perry Congrieve continued to talk for some time for Mark felt a stirring of interest in the young man despite his firm belief now that he had wrongly accused Judith of disloyalty.

'How is your wife, by the way?' Perry asked suddenly, 'I expect she's told you that we used to know each other.'

Mark nodded. 'Yes. She's very well, thanks.' He was a little curt for he did not choose to discuss Judith with this self-possessed young man.

Perry laughed. 'I promised to look her

up when I came over,' he said. 'I hope she doesn't throw me out on my ear. I wasn't exactly in her good books when we last met.' He added, offering his cigarette case, 'But, of course, she will have told you about that.'

Mark took a cigarette with a nod of thanks. 'A little,' he admitted.

Perry studied Mark with a trace of curiosity in his eyes. So this was the husband who owned Judith's obvious devotion. On the way over from Paris, Perry had been in two minds about seeing Judith again. He wanted to see her, if only once more, for the second experience of love had left a deeper impression than the first and he could not erase her from his heart and memory. But he took life philosophically and knowing she was unattainable he had consoled himself with other attractive women and knew the past was best left alone.

Now he said lightly: 'I was a little worried about her. You're sure the shock of the accident didn't affect her later—sometimes it has a delayed action, as you probably know.'

Mark stared at him. 'Accident?'

Perry drained his glass and snapped his fingers at the bar-tender. 'But of course. Surely Judith told you...' He stubbed his cigarette in a nearby ashtray, trying not to betray his surprise. 'That's one night of my life I'll never be able to account for,' he went on slowly. 'One minute we were careering down this tiny lane—the next I came round in a convent of all places, some hours later.' He paused and looked at Mark a little strangely. 'If Judith didn't mention the accident, how did she account for that night, Debenham? Or is that too personal a question?' he added slyly.

'Yes, it is,' Mark told him. Relief flooded him for although he had assured himself that Judith was innocent of anything but a flirtation with the Congrieve boy, the story he heard now doused the very last flicker of doubt in his heart. 'I'd like to hear more about this accident, Congrieve,' he said pleasantly, as the bar-tender placed fresh drinks before them. 'What actually happened?'

So at last the full story came out. With the relief came also shame that he had doubted her so much. Perry told the story well for he was a born *raconteur* and by the time it was finished, the two men were on excellent terms. Mark was his most charming self for he felt that he had also misjudged Congrieve who was, at the very worst, a romantic and a flirt who had snatched at the opportunity to recapture nostalgic memories.

Perry found himself liking Mark Debenham, despite the conviction that he would find him a prosy bore, typically English in that he was more concerned with business than the welfare of his wife. He was imbued with enough Continental sentiment to sigh a little for the complete loss of Judith for her husband was undoubtedly in love with her—the evidence was in his eyes and expression and his voice when he spoke Judith's name.

They talked for some while before Mark reluctantly took his farewell. Both being familiar with Paris, they naturally discussed her beauties, her femininity and her art treasures. Mutual friends too cropped up in conversation and it seemed surprising that they had never met through one or other of them.

When Mark left the Club, he drove directly to the block of luxury flats where Judith was staying with her friend. He had returned to Town the previous day and had telephoned the flat but Judith had been out. Without leaving a message, he had hung up for he decided that a telephone conversation would be too difficult. Far better to arrive at the flat and surprise her by his unexpected arrival. How would she receive him? With the swift happiness shining in her eyes—or with cold anger and a refusal to discuss the situation? This had been his decision before he met

Perry Congrieve: his talk with the young man had made no difference to his feelings concerning Judith except strengthened his resolve to heal the breach between them without further delay.

Judith herself answered the peal of the bell. She stepped back in surprise to see Mark but she opened the door wide and invited him to enter. At sight of him, the colour had surged into her cheeks, enhancing her natural beauty, and Mark's heart beat the faster with the longing to take her into his arms. But he carefully schooled his expression, merely saying: 'I'm glad to find you in, Judith. I want to talk to you.'

'Of course,' she said quickly. She indicated the wide, comfortable settee. 'Do sit down, Mark.'

He shook his head. 'No, thanks.' His eyes were on her face and she looked up at him with curiosity tinging her expression. He found it difficult to put his thoughts into words and suddenly his love engulfed him so that he was unable to speak of it. Instead, he said abruptly: 'I suppose you've heard about Casey?' He drew out his cigarette case and offered it as he spoke.

Judith took a cigarette. 'Yes. It's wonderful news, Mark—' She turned away and ignited a table lighter, bending her head over the flame. 'I went to see him yesterday,' she went on lightly. 'He's under drugs so much though that he didn't talk very much.'

'He'll be able to go home before long, Keiller hopes,' Mark told her. He took a step towards her. 'But I didn't come here to talk about Casey. Judith—'

'Yes, Mark.' She raised her head.

'We can't go on like this,' he said quickly. 'I came to ask you... Will you come home, Judith?' The simple words stumbled from his lips and his heart was in his eyes.

Judith caught her breath sharply. 'You mean—you want me back, Mark?' she asked tremulously.

He nodded. 'Yes, I do. There's no happiness without you—I need you, Judith.' He moved to take her hands. 'I can't bear this loneliness any longer.' There was a plea in his voice.

Judith longed to nestle into his arms and know the security of his nearness but pride pricked her and she remembered how much he had hurt her. She drew her hands away and without looking at him, she said bitterly: 'Don't you find Caroline an adequate antidote for loneliness?'

He gave an impatient gesture. 'Caroline? My dear Judith!'

'What else am I to think?' she demanded. 'You seem to be on excellent terms!'

He sat down and crossed his legs comfortably. Quizzically, he looked up at her. 'If you're thinking of the other day, I can offer you a very good explanation for my appointment with Caroline.'

'I'm not interested in your explanation,'

she taunted him and with a final shrug he accepted the reminder.

'Look here, Judith—I came to ask you to give our marriage another chance. Caroline has nothing to do with it. We're good friends and nothing more.'

'So you've told me before.' There was a faint sneer behind the words. 'Does Caroline believe it—any more than I do.'

His mouth tautened. 'What Caroline chooses to think is no fault of mine,' he said coolly. 'I've never encouraged her to care for me.'

'Then you do know that she's in love with you?'

He laughed. 'She's fancied herself in love with me for years, Judith. I've never worried about it—and I don't intend to start now. My own concern is for our happiness. Why not sit down and discuss it sensibly?'

'Sensibly!' She nearly cried the word. 'You're always so damned practical, Mark! Why can't you realize that one has to have a certain amount of romance in any marriage?'

'I do realize it,' he said slowly. 'For a long time I've known that my original attitude to marriage was totally wrong.' His voice changed. Rising to his feet, he came close to her and put his hands on her shoulders. 'Judith—do you still love me?' he asked. He was not ashamed of the urgency in his voice for it was the vital question which had worried him.

She walked away from him to the open window and stood looking down on the green square, the flocking birds, the passing traffic. In a quiet voice, she said: 'If I thought you loved me, Mark, I would try again. But we tried marriage once on the foundation of my love for you—it wasn't enough. It proved to me that marriage must be based on mutual love.' Her tone was suddenly harsh. 'I forgot my pride when you asked me to marry you—you told me then that love didn't come into it on your part. But now my pride is back, Mark—and I want no more of your pity!'

She turned to look at him soberly and he sensed the new maturity in her, a maturity born of pain and hurt pride and a staunch love.

Across the room, their eyes met and his were very honest. 'Judith, I married you because I loved you,' he said slowly. 'It took me some time to realize it and that's my main regret because it meant that we made a bad beginning to our life together. Now, I want you to come home with me because I love you—because my life is empty without you.'

There was a long silence as she searched his face. At last, she acknowledged the truth of his words and with a little sigh she moved towards him. He put his arms around her and drew her close.

'My darling—give me the chance to give you the happiness you deserve,' he pleaded.

She stood very still in his arms and her

heart was full. She had hoped and prayed for such a chance yet now that it was here she was hesitant and tremulous, fearful of the future.

'I love you,' he whispered against her lips and the ardent sincerity broke down the barrier she had strived to keep in place. Her lips welcomed his and their kiss was sweet and satisfying. He was reluctant to release her and she welcomed his nearness. With his cheek against her golden hair, he said suddenly: 'Judith, can you forgive me? I know the truth now and I'm sincerely sorry that I was such a hasty, hot-tempered fool.'

She drew away slightly and looked up at him.

'You've talked to Casey?'

He shook his head. 'No. How long has he known about the accident?'

'I told him the other day. Then—if not Casey, who, Mark?'

'Congrieve.'

Her eyes were startled. 'Perry? You've

seen him? Where? When?'

'He's in England on holiday. I met him, of all places, at my Club. He sought an introduction and we talked of many things—including you.' She had tensed in his arms and he held her closer. 'He was astonished to find that I knew nothing of that stupid car crash.'

Her lips trembled. 'Then that explains why you want me back, Mark. You believe Perry Congrieve—but you wouldn't listen to me. Now you know the truth, you've decided that after all I'm worthy to be your wife...'

He kissed her quickly to stop the spate of words. 'He had nothing to do with my decision, darling,' he told her. 'I wanted you back on any terms and believe me, it wouldn't have mattered if Congrieve had confirmed that you were with him that night. It's all in the past—and I love you too much.' He kissed her again. 'You haven't given me an answer yet,' he reminded her softly. 'Do you still love me?

Will you come home?'

It was natural that she should wonder in her heart if Mark would have asked these questions if he hadn't spoken to Perry. But she couldn't doubt that he loved her when the truth shone from his eyes and trembled on his lips when he kissed her. Her heart was suddenly light and she was filled with the knowledge of her love for him. A second chance with mutual love as a foundation would surely bring them happiness.

She nodded and said: 'Yes, I love you, Mark.' She impulsively kissed him and added: 'I'll go and pack my things, darling.'

Judith took very little time to pack for the majority of her possessions were still at Hurleigh. Mark waited, smoking a cigarette, looking about him at the small but excellently furnished flat, approving the occasional picture which hung on the walls, his thoughts busy with ways in which to atone to Judith and make her happy.

He telephoned the gallery to cancel all his appointments for the next few days and then they set off for home.

Judith smiled happily at Mark as he turned his head to glance at her by his side. Now, he thought, she was in her rightful place and he was determined that she should never stray from his side again. He turned his eyes back to the ribbon of road which stretched before them. As she studied his handsome profile she felt the familiar lurch of love and longing once again. His capable hands rested lightly on the wheel, the gold ring which he always wore gleaming in the bright sunshine.

She glanced down at her own hands, clasped in her lap. Her wedding ring, the wide gold band which was the symbol of the marriage tie, and which was her most valued possession. The diamonds of her engagement ring flashed and sparkled when she moved her fingers.

The sun streamed through the windows of the car to fall on her golden beauty.

Summer sunshine bathed the world with glory all about them. A surge of thankfulness rose in Judith's heart that love had saved their lives from matrimonial disaster and she knew a profound joy of living as happiness welled up within her. There were no doubts now. The knowledge that Mark loved her was enough for Judith and she gladly forgave and forgot the past.

They reached Hurleigh in what must have been record time for Mark was impatient with the road and eager to take Judith into his arms in the quiet peace of their home. They talked little but they were conscious of each other's presence and occasionally Mark's fingers sought Judith's hand with gentle pressure. She sensed his quiet contentment, the fullness of his heart and the words which trembled unspoken behind his lips.

She was very tired when they reached the house, a weariness which owed a great deal to the tense excitement that lay deep in her heart. Mark ordered tea to be brought to the lounge at once.

Judith greeted Alexander with a warm smile and his eyes lit eagerly at sight of her. His 'Welcome home, Madam—welcome home!' was sincere and Judith thrilled to the warmth in his voice. He bustled off to impart the good news to Sarah that Madam was home again and that the master's solicitous concern for her must mean an end to the recent strained atmosphere in the house.

Judith sat down in one of the armchairs and Mark gave her a cigarette. She lay back against the soft cushion and sighed her contentment. Mark stood by the hearth, looking down at her, and he knew that this lovely room held no greater treasure than the sweet beauty of his wife. Hours in the sun at Pelham had given her lovely skin a soft golden tan and brightened the gold in her hair: radiance lent a bloom to her cheeks and deepened the blue of her eyes. Her smile was sunnier than the rays which invaded the big room and the sweetness in her expression defied description.

Judith studied Mark with tender eyes. She thought again how handsome he was and how much she loved him. He could be hard and cruel, enigmatic and aloof—yet these faults no longer seemed to matter. Understanding and love could overcome them. He was kind and gentle, warm and loving beneath the cynical veneer—and these virtues were all-important to the wife who loved him deeply.

He was silent and she wondered at his thoughts. She held out a hand to him. 'Come and kiss me, Mark,' she invited in a low voice.

He threw his cigarette into the hearth where it smouldered unheeded until it finally burnt out. Bending his head, he touched her lips gently with his own, while he gripped her hands with ardent pressure and reassurance. 'Happy now?' he whispered against her sweetly-curved mouth.

She nodded. 'Very happy to be home,' she told him radiantly. 'Happier still to know that you really love me, Mark,' she added in a tender voice.

An agony of regret tore through him. 'I've been such a fool,' he said with anguish in his voice.

She touched his cheek with a gentle caress. 'It's over now,' she murmured. 'Let's forget everything, Mark—and really make a fresh start.'

'How can I ever forget the pain I caused you?' he asked bitterly.

'Darling, forget it,' she urged. 'I love you—and I don't want the rest of our lives marred by thoughts of the past.' She added ruefully: 'It was all my fault for deceiving you in the first place, anyway. How silly I was to think that you would prevent me from meeting an old friend! I've learnt my lesson now, Mark—I'll never lie to you again.'

'I've learnt several lessons,' he said unsteadily. 'To control my hasty temper, to give you the benefit of the doubt, to love you always and to tell you so often.'

'Hush! Don't speak of it any more.' She laid her fingers against his lips and he kissed them. 'It's over now,' she repeated but a little sigh escaped her when she recalled the suffering and her own silly deceit.

'How could I ever doubt your loyalty and your love when you always proved it in so many ways?' he said painfully.

They were interrupted by the arrival of Alexander carrying the tea-tray with its heavy silverware and the delicate china. Mark straightened up but his eyes never left Judith's face while they revealed his love and his repentance.

Judith busied herself with the tea-things for her heart was very full and tears sparkled behind the golden lashes. She struggled for control but one bright gem splashed on to her hand and then Mark took the cup from her, placed it firmly on the tray and drew her to her feet. She obediently went into the security of his arms and pressed her cheek against the roughness of his shoulder, while his lips touched the bright gold of her hair and they were close without words.

His expression was very serious as he thought over the last few months and realized how near they had come to losing the love which now flowed between them, erasing all past bitterness and anger. With the renewal of their love had come understanding—the precious gift which healed so swiftly the breach of pain and unhappiness which deceit had brought between them.

Mark understood now what had driven his young wife to deceit and he resolved that in future she should always be able to confide in him. Never again would his hasty temper preclude explanation of her actions and he knew that Judith would never again do anything which might cause him pain or anger.

Judith understood too the pain he had

known and she could appreciate that because love had come late to him, it was even more precious and the fear of losing her love had been more violent than his anger and the motive for his lack of compassion and kindness. Later, he had feared that he had killed her love through his harshness. Blaming himself, he had decided to offer Judith her freedom so that she should not be forced to go on living with a man she could not love.

But Mark appreciated their present happiness all the more and his sweet and lovely wife seemed infinitely dearer now they had overcome misunderstanding and pain. He could not deny that she had proved him far from immune to love and its manifold blessings. As he held her close and the evening sun crowned them both with roseate glory, he knew he could not live without the warmth in his heart that was his love for Judith.

CHAPTER XII

Casey lay on the comfortable garden-seat
on the lawn, a cushion behind his head,
a cigarette dangling from long fingers.
Though he was home again and suffered
no more pain, he still had to rest frequently
and long. But Casey was a tamed character
these days, obeying his nurse's instructions
without protest. But then, with such an
attractive nurse to care for him, it was
unlikely that he would defy her gently-
spoken orders.

She sat near him on the grass, not at
all starched or professional in her pink
candy-striped cotton dress, the sunshine
enhancing the richness of her dark-brown
curls, her fingers nimble as she stitched
away at a piece of embroidery.

A radio played, mingling music with the

song of the birds. While Casey soaked up the glory and splendour of the classical music which was among his favourites, his eyes rested on the girl and his expression was tender.

He lay looking at her for a long time and he knew a peace and contentment in his heart. At last he tired of looking and he took a cigarette from the packet beside him and aimed it at the crop of short curls. He aimed well and she looked up with a light laugh. 'Thank you, Casey,' she said demurely and put the cigarette between her lips.

'That was meant to attract your attention —not to be smoked,' he told her gaily.

She rose and moved to his side. She had an easy natural grace of movement and Casey watched her approvingly. He flicked his lighter into flame and she bent her head over it. Then she threw her head back, letting the smoke wreathe up about her head, her eyes laughing at Casey. 'Do you want anything?' she asked lightly.

'Yes. Talk to me, will you?' he said in reply.

She shrugged. 'What shall I talk about? Give me a subject and I'll oblige.'

His eyes twinkled. 'Well, we could talk about you. What do you intend to do when Sir Martin decides that I don't need you any more?'

At the end of the few weeks which Dr Kahn had prophesied, the pain which Casey lived with abated a great deal. Sir Martin had decided to send him home to Hurleigh but nothing would please Casey but that Ann Davenport should accompany him as the nurse he would need for a few weeks. Sir Martin had agreed, for the shrewd, kindly man felt sure that the young man would make better progress if he could have his own way on this point.

Ann was very happy at the Lodge and Casey's words were a reminder that one day she would have to leave. She had swiftly fallen in love with Hurleigh, the big attractive house and the lovely surrounding countryside. Judith and Mark liked the young nurse and had made her very welcome much to Casey's pleasure. It was an interesting life at the Lodge for many of Casey's friends called to entertain him: occasionally Mark drove Casey and Ann up to the Ancells for the day; there was plenty to do at the Lodge itself and Casey was not a demanding patient. But Ann most enjoyed to be with him.

It had been a great relief and a joy to everyone that Casey would not suffer for the rest of his life from the unfortunate fall. Sir Martin gladly gave all the credit to Kahn and promised Casey that if all went well he would be a fit man again within six months.

It had been wonderful to Casey to find that the pain gradually abated, that he regained gradual movement in his limbs and grew stronger with every passing day. He attributed his peace of mind and patience to Ann for the new love had completely erased the memory of the old and he thought of Judith now with only the warm affection of a brother to a much-loved sister. He was grateful that Ann was readily accepted by both Mark and Judith, not realizing that they appreciated Ann's good influence on the wild young man with his restless moods and the sensitive dreamy nature.

The knowledge that Mark and Judith were reconciled had helped a lot in Casey's recovery—or so he assured them, insisting that it was the best tonic he could have had to know that they were together again at the Lodge and filling the house with happiness. Mark's laughing reply had been to the effect that in his view Casey's best tonic was Ann for she knew how to handle him.

They were the best of friends and Judith often exchanged glances with Mark when their light-hearted banter went back and forth and their laughter mingled on the summer air.

Now Ann said slowly: 'Oh, I shall stick to private nursing, in future, I think. It's more interesting.' She sat down on the grass beside him and hugged her knees. After a moment, she added with a break in her voice: 'The only snag is that one gets fond of a patient which makes the eventual parting very hard.'

He put a hand on her shoulder. She was glad that her face was turned away from him because her love leaped into her eyes and she thrilled to his touch.

'Will it be hard to leave me?' he asked softly. His hand strayed to the rich brown curls and he stroked them affectionately. He waited for the answer with thudding heart.

She nodded. 'Very hard,' she replied with a lump in her throat. She felt his lips touch her hair and she turned to him quickly. His arms went around her and then his lips were tender and sweet against her responsive mouth.

For a long moment there was silence.

It was their first kiss, despite their close friendship, the easy intimacy and the love which both knew and yet which still had not been confessed.

He smiled into her serious face. 'I've been wanting to do that for weeks, Ann girl,' he said slowly and kissed her again, regardless of the reproachful eyes of Pilgrim, the Alsatian, who rose on his haunches and growled with jealousy. He was conscious only of the nearness of the girl he loved and the sweetness of her lips.

Mark stood at the window of the lounge and he was smiling. He turned to speak to Judith who was arranging flowers for a table decoration.

He said dryly: 'From all appearances, Casey is almost well again. He seems to be his old self now, anyway.'

Judith looked up from her task. 'Yes,' she agreed, although she had not witnessed the scene which so amused Mark. 'He doesn't really need Ann any longer. I guess he just likes to have her around.'

Mark chuckled. 'Come and see for yourself if he needs her or not!' he invited. She went to stand by his side and he slipped his arm about her shoulders.

Casey held Ann very close still and they were oblivious to everything but themselves. Judith smiled up at Mark and then turned away, reluctant to overlook the intimacy of the little scene.

'Ann won't want to leave when Casey is really well again,' she said slowly. 'I think she's in love with him.'

Mark nodded. 'I agree. I would say that Casey is also smitten but I'm not sure if he's serious or whether he means to part with her in due course and call it *finis!*'

'He couldn't do that!' Judith exclaimed sharply. 'It would be too cruel. If he doesn't love her—doesn't want to marry her, then he should send her away now and certainly not indulge in that kind of thing!' With the last words she waved a hand in the direction of the lawn.

Mark shrugged. 'I think he's waiting to be really sure. Casey's like that. Wild and impetuous he may be but when something serious crops up, he likes to take his time and think things over carefully. One day, he'll be sure—and I think we'll lose him to little Ann Davenport.'

'Do you mind?' Judith asked slowly.

'Not at all. She's a sweet girl and I like her very much. The main thing, of course, is Casey's happiness. And she's proved she can handle him capably—I've never known him so docile.'

'As long as she doesn't subdue him too much,' Judith said. 'Casey wouldn't be our Casey without some gaiety and recklessness!'

'I don't think there's much fear of that,' Mark replied. He added. 'Tell me, Judith—was there ever a time when Casey meant anything to you?'

The question startled her. She did not answer for a moment while she finished her task with the flowers. Then she turned and went to him, putting her arms about him, looking up into his face with a sunny smile. 'Darling, I can't remember a time when Casey didn't mean a lot to me. I'm devoted to him, I love him dearly, and I shall be very pleased if he marries Ann and finds all the happiness he deserves so much.'

'That isn't what I mean,' he said slowly, feeling that she had neatly evaded the searching question.

She laughed lightly, strained on her toes to kiss his chin. Then she said teasingly: 'Old Man Jealousy seems to be raising his ugly head again, Mark, my dear. Why are you unsure of me, darling? Don't you believe that I love you with all my heart, that I always have and I always will?'

He drew her close. 'I try to believe,' he said quietly and she was touched by the simplicity of his reply. 'But sometimes I remember how wonderful you are and it's beyond my comprehension that you should love a man like me.'

To hide the emotion his words roused in her, she said lightly: 'Modesty isn't in your line, darling! I do love you—but I haven't time now to go into all my reasons.'

He released her and she smoothed the sleek golden chignon which still crowned her proud head, adding elegance to beauty. She bent to pat Digger who licked her fingers eagerly, swiftly aroused from sleep at the touch of her caressing hand.

Judith set out for the village some minutes later with Digger at her heels. As she passed Casey and Ann, now apart but talking with animation, she waved to them and they returned the greeting. The walk did not take long and she made her purchases, stopping for a few minutes to talk to an occasional villager. On the way back, she walked briskly, enjoying the exercise. It was such a lovely afternoon that she had felt a real need to be out in the fresh air and sunshine, leaving Mark to write letters in his study.

As she passed the Mallows house, she

automatically glanced towards it and saw that Caroline's car stood in the drive. So she was home again. She had been amazingly restless these last few months and could not settle in Hurleigh for more than a few days at a time. Allan jogged along by himself in a pleasant way for he was a man who liked his own company, was a born bachelor and valued his freedom. He much preferred to please his own tastes and do as he wished rather than have to buckle to someone else's whims. His housekeeper looked after him excellently, he had his friends and his hobbies, and Judith had often wondered if it were not a relief to him when Caroline took herself off to London or the Continent for weeks at a time.

Caroline's car passed her when she was walking up the drive of the Lodge and the klaxon sounded a greeting. Judith waved in response.

To her surprise, Sir Martin Keiller was waiting with Caroline by the main door for her to reach them. His dark eyes were quick to appraise her golden good looks, the chic elegance of the blue suit she wore and the ready smile she gave them both.

Despite the jealousy she had once entertained where Caroline was concerned, Mark had dispelled all this with his evident love and loyalty, so Judith could greet the woman with real warmth.

They entered the house together and Mark came out of the study, hearing the voices. His face creased in a smile as he came forward to greet the visitors.

Sir Martin said: 'We're actually killing two birds with one stone, Debenham. I'd like to have a look at Casey—and also Caroline and I wanted to break the news of our marriage.'

There was a surprised silence then Mark said quickly: 'Congratulations! I'm very pleased and wish you both all the happiness in the world.'

Judith added her own congratulations and then they entered the lounge where Mark dispensed drinks all round.

'Well, you're a dark horse, Caroline!' he accused, handing her a drink. 'When were you married?'

'Three days ago,' she replied smoothly. 'Martin has been pressing me to marry him for a long time—I finally gave in with a good grace.' She flashed a laughing glance at the tall figure of her husband. Having at last acknowledged defeat where Mark was concerned, she had turned her attentions to Martin Keiller. They had been friends for some years and he had suggested marriage several times. Love might not be the ruling factor of the alliance but they understood each other and were confident of a tolerable amount of happiness in the future.

Meanwhile, Ann and Casey had decided their own future. Drawing away from his arms, she had tidied her hair with a trembling hand. She was confused and little dismayed at the warmth she had found in his kisses yet the love in her heart was glad to find a response. Casey's heart was thudding uncomfortably and the nerves in his stomach were tense. He told himself ruefully that he was reacting like a boy of sixteen to the situation. He had determined when Ann was in his arms that he wanted to marry her yet the usually-confident Casey feared a refusal.

Abruptly, he said: 'You don't have to leave, Ann girl. You could marry me and give up nursing.'

She turned a startled face to him with the joy breaking through the amazement. Bantering, she replied: 'Do you think that career would suit me better than nursing?'

He grinned. 'I can offer excellent prospects,' he assured her lightly.

She pursed her lips while her eyes laughed down at him. 'I'm not worried about the prospects,' she said easily, 'but I do think the employer might be a little difficult to manage.'

He drew her close with a sudden movement and kissed her soundly. 'You've proved often enough that you know how to handle him,' he whispered against her soft cheek. 'I love you, Ann girl. Will you marry me?'

She gave a little nod. 'Yes, I will, my boy,' she said in a firm voice and kissed him. 'I don't make a habit of falling in love with my patients but now I've got the awful disease, I suppose marriage is the only cure!'

They took little notice of the arrival of the car for they were deep in animated conversation, discussing their future and the marriage which Casey insisted should not be too long in taking place. Ann's only request was that they should wait until Sir Martin told him he was really fit again.

It was a surprise when Sir Martin himself came across the lawn towards them with Mark, Caroline and Judith close behind him. A greater surprise still when they were informed that Sir Martin and Caroline were newly married. A great smile lit Casey's face.

'Just to be in the fashion,' he said gaily, 'Ann and I are engaged!'

Mark and Judith exchanged laughing glances. Then Judith said: 'That's no surprise—one's enough in one day! But how glad I am to hear of it, Casey!' She went to him and kissed his cheek, then she turned to hug Ann and say: 'I'm so happy for you, Ann!'

The others exchanged congratulations and Mark said dryly: 'I can't think of a better wife for you, Casey. Perhaps you'll take more care of yourself in future...'

'Not at all!' Casey interrupted. 'With a qualified nurse for a wife, I can be as reckless as ever.'

'And probably will be,' Mark said with a laugh. He turned to Judith and said: 'We must ask Sarah to produce the best dinner possible at such short notice and send Alexander to the cellar for champagne. This calls for a celebration—it's about time Casey was off my hands for good.' He turned to Sir Martin and his wife.

'You'll dine with us, I hope?'

The dinner party was a great success that evening. They were a small but happy party and the atmosphere was gay with quips and banter and much laughter.

Happiness was evident in Casey's shining eyes and the sweet curve of Ann's lips: love flowed between them like an invisible bond which kept them close though they sat apart and behaved outwardly as though getting engaged was an everyday occurrence in their lives.

Judith could not help but envy them. They were not afraid to betray their youthful love and the happiness which sprang from newness of the knowledge of their mutual love. But while she envied them, she would not have turned back the clock for herself and Mark, for Judith realized that they had reached a vale of contentment where past problems and difficulties were only a background to present happiness and peace of mind.

Mark glanced across at Judith. The black

velvet of her evening gown accentuated her slim fairness: diamonds sparkled at her throat and in her ears; happiness shone from her eyes and vibrated in her voice. For once, the chignon was loosened and the shining gold of her hair nestled against the creaminess of her throat and shoulders. She looked very young and ethereal. Mark was suddenly filled with pride of possession for such beauty touched the very core of his sensitive being. It was not surprising that he loved this wife of his so much—she was his most valued possession and her love was the most precious gift he could ever hope to receive. A gift that every lucky possessor should guard zealously for it is too easily lost when misunderstanding and doubt and pain arise.

Judith looked up and met his eyes and the glance she gave him was meant for him alone to read and understand. Though Casey and Ann had a vision of happiness and the natural elation of newly-discovered love, she had the knowledge that her marriage was proving both successful and happy despite the unsteadiness of its course some months earlier. They had weathered that storm at last and Judith's eyes assured Mark that she would never want any other pilot in life but him and that her love was his for ever.

So she smiled across at him and in reply he raised his glass of champagne to her in an almost imperceptible toast and his eyes spoke eloquently of the fullness in his heart.